ON THE WINGS OF MURDER

FLORIDA KEYS BED & BREAKFAST COZY MYSTERY
BOOK THREE

DANIELLE COLLINS

Fairfield Publishing

CONTENTS

"OH, that's perfect. Don't move." Eva Stewart bit her lip as she tried to put her friends in focus, turning the lens back and forth. "Uh, just one more adjustment—"

"Are you planning on taking the photo *this* century?" Pete Jenkins asked through clenched teeth. He was supposed to be smiling, but it looked more like a grimace.

"I…just…there."

Click.

Eva pulled the camera away to examine her work, but her expression fell. Blurry. Again.

"Well?" Kay Jenkins asked, stepping from her husband's side to get a peek at the picture, their pet grooming business behind them as a backdrop. "Oh."

"Sorry." Eva let out a sigh. "I suppose I'll just need to practice a bit more."

"We're happy to be your guinea pigs." Pete rolled his eyes and gave a weak smile.

Kay laughed. "He may sound put out, but don't let that

bother you. We really don't mind. Some new photos of us in front of the business will be good for marketing."

"Maybe you should hire someone who actually knows what they're doing." Eva shrugged her shoulders.

"You're just learning," Kay said, putting a motherly hand on her shoulder. "You'll get it."

"Thanks," Eva said, slipping her large digital camera into a padded bag. "But today is not the day that happens."

"Want to come in for coffee?" Pete asked.

"No, but thank you. I think I'll take a walk."

"It is a lovely day, though a bit hot," Kay commented.

Eva didn't mind the warmer weather, but as the humidity continued to spike, it did hold less of an appeal. Thankfully, today it was mild, and she looked forward to a walk along the beach not too far from the Jenkin's business and home.

"Here." Pete came out of the shop with a chilled bottle of water. "For the walk."

"Thank you."

"And really…" Pete smiled back at her. "You can take our photos anytime. Hope I didn't give you too hard of a time."

"Nonsense," she said, smiling back at her friends. "See you on Friday?"

"We'll be there," Kay said.

Waving, Eva stepped out of the gate, making sure to close it securely behind her. There were always dogs or other animals roaming their yard, and she didn't want to be the cause of one getting out.

Eva hitched her bag up higher on her shoulder and

walked down the street, making a left to a narrow trail she knew led to the beach. The sun was high above since it was just past one o'clock, and the wind was sure to be stiffer on the beach. She wouldn't mind that since the camera equipment was a little heavier than she'd anticipated and likely wouldn't bounce around against her hip.

While Eva was used to spending most of her days at her bed-and-breakfast, The Key's, and hosting a murder mystery book club with various friends, she had recently felt the itch to try something new.

Some of her friends had blamed Eva's new obsession with photography on a new case she wasn't sharing with them. She had truthfully reassured them that her new hobby had nothing to do with solving crimes and everything to do with trying something new.

The crime solving had fallen into her lap on several occasions now, but she couldn't count on something like that to keep cropping up. It had been quite satisfying to solve the murder of an intellectual property thief, as well as the murder of a well-known, wealthy man named Charles Wodehouse only a few months ago. Not to mention that her bed-and-breakfast had been infiltrated by reporters pretending to be a couple. In reality, they'd just wanted to follow her to gain information about the largest case Key West had seen in many years.

But that was more than enough excitement for one year, and now Eva was on the search for excitement of another kind. That of finding the perfect shot to frame.

She stepped from the cover of the bushes out onto the

open beach, the sand slipping past her sandals and covering her toes in warmth even as the wind whipped her shoulder-length red hair in front of her eyes.

Eva took a moment to secure her hair back and then trudged through the deep sand to the firmer ground near the waves. Warm as it was, the wind still held a hint of chill coming off the water, and she enjoyed it while the sun beat down on her with its unflinching heat.

There were no clouds to be seen, just what felt like an endless beach with early vacationers or residents soaking up some sun on the sand. It was picturesque and stirred something inside of Eva. A longing to capture the feeling through a photo.

Without much hope of success, Eva pulled out her camera again. She changed lenses to a wider angle and positioned herself to frame the water and the beach, giving the water more space in the shot to balance the endless blue sky.

Taking a careful accounting of her settings and trying desperately to recall what she'd learned from the book she was reading, she set the aperture and shutter speed and pressed her finger down.

Click.

This time when she pulled the camera back to take in her work—the anticipation making her heart beat faster—she was surprised to see she'd captured exactly what she wanted!

"Why can't I do that with people?" she mumbled to herself.

Sighing, she put the camera back to her eye and shifted

a little. She featured the businesses lining the beach several hundred feet away, a few children playing in the sand, and then a man walking his dog by the ocean. She was careful not to get clear images of anyone's face, not wanting to infringe on their privacy. Then again, she knew no one would see these images since they were just for her.

Each photo turned out close to what she'd intended. Oh sure, some were a little too bright, but she'd read where there were programs that could fix that. Happier than she'd been when she left Kay and Pete, Eva headed down the beach with renewed excitement.

The wind brought the scent of salt, and she breathed in deeply. It was nice to take time to enjoy where she'd lived. With the cases she'd worked alongside her book club and the new-to-town detective Jerome Makos, she had found it difficult to truly relax in the last few months.

It was telling that, while it had been almost two months since the last case, she still hadn't fully let her guard down. How could she when these cases had all but fallen into her lap?

She raised her camera and took a shot of a man staring out toward the sea. He had a pensive look on his face under the deep brim of a straw hat, but something about him struck a memory in Eva.

UNCLE SAL SAT with his back to the ocean, staring out. A camera to the side of him, his eyes scanned the beach like a cat looking for a mouse. Ever watchful. Tense.

"Can we get ice cream now?" young Eva asked.

"Soon, honey. Just need to catch—there he is."

Uncle Sal lifted his camera up, placing his eye to the eyepiece and clicking away.

Young Eva watched where his camera pointed, but she couldn't see anything.

"What are ya taking pictures of, Uncle Sal?"

He took several more shots, the camera lens following the subject across the beach, before he put the camera down, slipping it back into its case.

"All right, pumpkin, let's get that ice cream."

EVA BLINKED out of her memory and kept walking along the beach, but she could still remember the way her Uncle Sal had looked. Focused. On the job. Ready to do what it took, but he'd still made time for her.

Some might have thought it was odd he'd brought his niece along for the ride while trailing a suspect for his private investigation business, but she'd loved every minute.

Eva treasured the intrigue of days spent with her uncle on 'assignments' as he'd called them. She'd learned a lot from him, even going so far as to consider a career as a private investigator when she grew into her teen years and beyond, but her lawyer father and wealthy mother scoffed at the idea.

In the end, she'd studied business management and international relations, though she'd never fully gotten past the bug of investigation. Perhaps that was why she was so invested in the cases she'd helped with in Key West.

Taking a few more shots, Eva reached another trail that would take her back to the main street and on home to her bed-and-breakfast. Pausing at the mouth to the trail, she carefully tucked her camera back into her bag and zipped it up.

If she'd learned anything that day, it was that she might be better at landscapes than portrait photography. And that was fine by her.

———

"HOLA, DULZURA."

"Hello, Ruben," Eva answered into the phone later that afternoon. She'd showered, uploaded her photos to her computer, and was now sitting at her desk in the main area of the Key's Bed and Breakfast doing paperwork for the business and working on her summer bookings. It was June, but school was letting out and things were promising to get busier and busier.

"Did I catch you at a bad time?"

She clicked through to another page of the planning software her employee, Jake, had created for them.

"Um, not exactly. I'm working on some bookings. It's getting busy."

"Time to expand, eh?"

She laughed. "You wouldn't let me. Besides, I can't seem to hire you to redo one room let alone build more for me."

"You wound me, *dulzura*. I would do anything for you."

She rolled her eyes at his dramatic fashion, but it was very 'Ruben' of him, so she let it slide. "Anything but the White Room."

"*Si*. It must remain *blanco*. It is the right choice. You'll thank me later."

Now she laughed out loud. "I'm changing up that room whether you like it or not, Ruben Vargas. Whether I use Vargas Construction or your competitor—that's up to you."

"You would not," he said, sounding like he was choking on air.

She paused, letting his fear linger for a brief moment. "I wouldn't. And you know it."

It was his turn to laugh. "We will talk of this 'White Room' later. What is more important now is *café*."

"Coffee?"

"You and I. We've been trying so hard to meet and it has not happened."

"Because you're too busy for your own good."

She clicked on a few separate boxes, making sure they corresponded with the emails she'd gotten. Some folks, especially those less advanced on computers, tended to email their requests rather than use the booking portal they'd installed several years ago. It was a challenge because sometimes those bookings overlapped, but she realized that not everyone understood the website, especially those who tended toward less technology and more in-person connections.

"Well?"

Ruben's comment drew her from her thoughts. "Well what?"

"You. Me. *Café*. Soon, *si?*"

"Yes." She pulled her gaze away from the computer screen. It wasn't right to divide her attention between work and her friend. "Soon."

"I will text you a date tonight or tomorrow, all right?"

"That sounds good. I'm looking forward to hearing about your trip."

"And I am looking forward to seeing you."

They said their goodbyes, and then Eva hung up to refocus on the computer work, but now her thoughts were distracted. Ruben had come back from visiting Cuba where his family still lived and had jumped right back into work. He was a contractor and ran his own construction company, so he'd had to jump on several projects that needed his immediate attention.

He'd said multiple times how much he wanted to reconnect with her since they'd missed their coffee date before his trip, and yet every time she tried to make an appointment with him, it had fallen through. For a month!

While Eva was busy herself, she'd also learned that delegating created a much better work and life balance. Then again, she'd known Ruben since she first moved to Key West over six years ago. He'd always been not only a hard worker, but a little micro-managing. She couldn't fault him, his name *was* the business, but still, it made times like these difficult.

The rest of Eva's afternoon went quickly, and she

managed to settle all of the booking which made her feel quite accomplished. After a quick dinner of fish and steamed vegetables, she settled into a poolside lounge chair she kept reserved for evenings just such as this.

The back of the bed-and-breakfast featured a lovely wide porch, part of which was separated by hanging curtains. The separation allowed Eva to have a secluded spot to enjoy her own yard, but the rest of the space was filled with comfortable chairs and lounges for guests.

Then, going down a set of four steps, also accessible by a ramp, guests had access to a rectangular pool with cool water and a separate hot tub, all under bistro lights strung overhead. There was a gas firepit, cushioned teak outdoor furniture, along with a station for towels and snacks. She's even added a mini-fridge for cold drinks.

There was nothing Eva loved more than seeing her guests enjoying the area, especially the children, but the quietness of an evening like this was her next favorite thing. Her guests were all younger that week, mostly business professionals taking some vacation time, and they all seemed to be out at the clubs which left her the secluded area to herself.

High above, past the city lights, she knew stars shown down, but all she could see were the glistening bistro lights reflected by the still water, all accompanied by the soothing sound of water falling over rocks from her fountain in the corner.

Two more days until their book club met and she still had several chapters to finish in the book they were reading. It was a murder mystery by a new-to-her author, and while she'd already guessed the ending, it was still interesting to see how it would all come out.

Taking a sip of her favorite drink—iced tea with a squeeze of fresh lime—she picked up her book and settled in for an evening of reading. To Eva, it was the most perfect way to enjoy an evening alone.

2

"WILL SOMEONE HAND ME A NAPKIN?"

"That's what you get for taking the last *three* key lime squares, Willard," Geraldine Walker said, eyeing him with a look that said she was not happy to help even though she was doing it anyway.

"No one else had taken them—" Willard Smith began his protest but stopped when Geraldine's look intensified.

"Because we've only *just* started our meeting! I was looking forward to enjoying at least one more of those delightful squares of heavenly, tart goodness but no, you had to go ahead and—"

"Not to worry," Eva said, butting into their argument. "I have more."

At Willard's hopeful look Geraldine held out a hand. "You've had your fill. And yes, I will tell Bonnie if you even think of taking one more. Five is plenty."

Willard had the decency to look bashful about his overindulgence, but Eva merely grinned. Bonnie,

Willard's wife, had warned Eva early on that Willard was on a diet, and while Eva did what she could, there was only so much policing of a grown man and his sweet tooth.

"And back to the book," Pete said, giving a look all around that said, *Remember, this is why we're here.*

"I will admit I liked the way she foreshadowed the killer," Kay said, heeding her husband's suggestion.

"You mean how she practically told us all who it was going to be in chapter two?" Geraldine looked unimpressed. "Sure, she can write, but I really think she should stick to romances. That was my favorite part of this book."

"It wasn't a romance," Vicky Clem said. She wore a bright pink dress and strappy white heels.

Once again, Eva found herself wondering how Key West's medical examiner always managed to keep her attire spotless.

"It kind of was," Elijah Tang said with a shrug.

"Sure, if you think it's romantic to be stalked by the real killer," Kay said, giving an exaggerated shiver.

"It was pretty creepy," Elijah admitted. He was picking at white paint on his nails. "But he was kind of nice."

"Until he tried to kill her," Kay added.

Trying to shift the conversation, Eva stepped in. "What did you all like about the ending?"

"That it was done," Geraldine said, making clear her feelings about the novel. A few snickered as she tossed the paperback onto the table. "But they can't all be Agatha Christie with Hercule Poirot."

"Pretty bird! Poirot gets a treat."

Everyone turned to stare at the large Amazon parrot sitting in his outdoor cage. He'd been relatively quiet up until that point, but now he spoke up when he heard his name, which was to be expected.

Poirot the Parrot was never one to let a murder mystery book club go without adding something—usually something hysterical—to their conversation.

"Sorry. I'll give him the treat," Geraldine said, looking a little guilty. In her seventies and wearing a long and flowing tunic with wedge sandals, the woman slipped out of the circle and over to the bird cage, talking to the parrot the whole time.

"I liked that we could sympathize with the murderer—to an extent," Elijah said, taking up Eva's question. "I mean, not that I'm a psychopath, but it's easy to connect with someone who has feelings for someone else, but they don't see you." Eva thought she might have imagined it, but had Elijah looked at Vicky after he spoke?

"True, but I found the police procedure to be a little off in this," Pete said. He was a big lover of true crime shows and often discussed how something wasn't realistic in fiction.

"Yes, but it made it more dramatic," Kay pointed out.

"True. Especially when the killer was able to get her to the top of that building before they knew where he'd gone—very scary to think of," Vicky added.

"I liked the food descriptions," Willard said.

For as serious as he'd been in making the statement, it was too on the nose for everyone who knew Willard's passion for food. They all burst into laughter, and it only grew louder at Willard's shock.

When things calmed down, they moved past the book and onto their next read. When they all settled on a new choice, Eva drew out her camera from behind her chair.

"Mind if I snap a picture everyone?"

Pete made a groaning sound, but then grinned back at her. "Just kidding."

They all shifted to the largest couch, with a few of them standing behind, while Eva lined up the shot. She'd been working on settings for just such a situation and hoped she'd get it right this time. At least more quickly than she had at Kay and Pete's. Of course, that had been around lunch time, and she'd read in her photography book that mid-day wasn't the best time for photos. Now, with golden sunlight fading in from the west, the photograph shouldn't be as washed out.

They all smiled as she called out to say cheese, and when she peeked at the photo, she was relatively happy with the results. "I think I got it."

"Good job," Kay said, ever the optimist and encourager.

"Speaking of photos," Elijah said, as everyone took their seats, "I have some fun news."

"Finally sell a painting?" Willard said, with sarcasm.

Elijah made a face at him, though the gesture was good-natured as they both enjoyed ribbing one another. "Actually," Elijah said, looking pleased with himself, "I'm going to be selling a lot of them. Or so I hope. I've got an art exhibit going in at The Pierson Gallery."

Everyone rushed to congratulate him, but the extra attention clearly embarrassed him. Elijah was a well-known modern artist who had gained popularity in the Bay Area of California, near San Francisco, but had chosen to move to Key West to pursue a different type of art instead. With a more impressionist feeling to his art these days, he'd struggled to find the same type of success as he had for his modern pieces, but slowly he was building up a fan base.

"The Pierson exhibit is a big deal," Eva said, reaching over to squeeze his shoulder. "That's incredible."

"I have to admit, I was pretty shocked." Now he looked a little sheepish. "They want me to display *both* types of my artwork."

"You're kidding," Vicky said.

"I know." He rolled his eyes. "But I decided to agree because both genres are me and I couldn't see logic in giving up a big opportunity like this just on the principle that I want my newest form to sell."

"That's smart. Take it as an advancement," Pete said.

"I'm trying."

Everyone discussed the opportunity as Eva brought out the last tray of key lime squares that she'd kept hidden away, and then the book club members began to head home.

"Eva," Elijah said, coming up to her after saying goodbye to Kay and Pete. "Could you do me a favor?"

"Anything."

Eva had met Elijah one day when she'd been walking the boardwalk where he was painting on an easel, looking out over the water. They'd struck up a conversation about their favorite murder mysteries, so she'd invited him to her small book club. Their friendship had only grown despite the difference in their ages—he was in his late thirties and she was in her late forties.

"Would you take some photos at the opening?" Elijah smiled.

She blinked. "Anything but that," she said with a laugh.

"Oh, come on, Eva."

"It's not that I don't want to help you," she explained quickly, "but I'm not very good. I've only *just* started learning."

"I don't want them for much more than sentimental value. You'd do that for me, wouldn't you?"

And there, looking up into his warm brown eyes, she knew she would do that. "All right. But I'm not promising professional quality."

"Deal," he said with a laugh before turning to go.

"What was that all about?" Vicky asked as she walked over from where she'd been talking with Geraldine.

"Elijah wants me to take some photos at the opening of his exhibit."

"Oh honey, that's great," Vicky said.

She had come to Key West from Houston, Texas and the twang of her accent came out more strongly at certain times, which always made Eva smile. They had become good friends over the last several months and Eva was so thankful for her friendship.

"It is, but I'm honestly not that good." Eva shrugged.

"I'm sure he's fine with that. Sounds like it's more for the memories than anything."

Eva nodded. "That's true."

"I'm excited for him," she said, watching as he helped Geraldine into her cab. "He's a good guy."

"He is," Eva said, her head tilting to the side as she observed her friend. "A very good guy."

"What?" Vicky said, looking back at Eva as her tone sunk in.

"Nothing. Just thinking that, if he's such a good guy, why did you turn down his offer to get coffee last week?"

"Wait…how did you know that?"

"He asked me if he'd made a mistake," Eva said. "He was afraid that he'd ruined your friendship."

"What did you tell him?" she asked.

"To ask you that."

Vicky rolled her eyes. "Oh Eva."

"Well, it's true, right? You're the only one who can answer that."

Vicky was quiet for a long time. "I like him. Like I said, he's a good guy, but there's a part of me that worries about just that. Ruining our friendship, the MMBC and everything," she said, referring to the Murder Mystery Book Club.

Eva took a moment to consider all of this, but then she simply said, "You won't know unless you try."

AFTER SEEING her friends off and cleaning up after them, which wasn't difficult since Geraldine always insisted on doing most of the work for her, Eva returned to her small cottage at the back of her property.

The Victorian home she'd purchased and remodeled into the bed-and-breakfast after her parent's untimely death hadn't come with the addition, but since her parents had left her a healthy sum of money, she decided to add an additional cottage where she could live separately from her guests.

Coming home every night to the one-bedroom cottage reminded her of what a good idea it had been to build it. While she loved being in the hospitality industry and had her phone as an emergency contact for any guests, she also enjoyed having her own space.

Tonight, the space felt cozy and just right. She'd made sure she'd turned the AC down a little lower than necessary so she could turn on her gas fireplace for a bit of before-bed reading. She knew it was an indulgent use of air-conditioning, but she didn't do it often, and tonight she'd really wanted a cozy atmosphere to help her unwind from the day.

While MMBC members always made her feel loved and cared for, she also found she was drained after such interactions. She was most certainly more of an introvert, but she also treasured time with her friends. It was a delicate balance.

Eva took a few minutes to tidy up the place, though there wasn't much she had to do, and then she grabbed a true crime novel she'd been reading at Pete's request. He knew they were a fictional book club, but he wanted her to see how sometimes non-fiction could read like fiction.

Truth be told, Eva felt like she'd lived enough true crime in the last several months, but she also appreciated Pete's dedication to the group and was going to push through the book.

She'd just taken her cup of chamomile tea to the coffee table and turned on the fireplace when her phone dinged. It was the sound of an email coming through.

Eva prided herself on being the type of person who wasn't tied to her phone. She found that she spent most of her day without needing it unless something came up for a guest or she had to make a call or send a text, but there was one weakness for her. Email.

It had started in school, and she'd carried the less-than-ideal habit through moving to Key West and starting up her business. She always felt compelled to check her email and respond as soon as possible to any requests.

Even now, it was foolish to worry about her email since this was her time to herself and nothing could be that pressing, but the little ding had triggered her innate desire to have a close-to-empty inbox.

Promising herself that she wouldn't spent more than two seconds checking who had sent the email—and that she would silence her phone after looking—she picked up her phone and swiped it open to check the preview window.

To: Eva Stewart <estewart@thekeysbandb.com>

From: <goodnitemoon536@xmail.com>
Subject: P.I. help needed

EVA FROWNED. She didn't recognize the sender, but the subject was intriguing. She tapped through, still promising herself that she wouldn't spend much time on this. It was likely a scam, and she certainly wouldn't tap through any links that the scammer might have added. The mere act of opening it wouldn't send a virus to her phone, right? Did phones even get viruses?

Seeing as she'd already opened the email, she decided to leave the questions—and perhaps ramifications—for when Jake came in the next day. For now, she'd read what the email had to say.

DEAR MS. STEWART,

I'm afraid I can't say who this is right now, but I'm in need of your help. You helped me once, and I'm reaching out for a favor yet again.

If you agree to help, please reply yes or no. Don't reply with details. I'll contact you again with a more secure way to interact.

IT SOUNDED SO CONFUSING. Almost as if the sender knew her, and yet they wouldn't give details. Other than that, it sounded like a scam. Like there was no way that it was a genuine email.

And yet the email address triggered some memory. The book Good Night Moon had been one of her favorites as a child, but surely there was no connection between that and the email address the sender had chosen, was there?

Eva swiped left and sent the email to the archive—wherever that went. She wasn't going to spend another minute trying to figure out a piece of spam mail.

Turning her phone on silent, knowing important calls would still get through, she set it face down on the coffee table and picked up her book. The plot was thickening as the detectives drew near to the perpetrator. Eva was instantly sucked into the story. When she looked at the clock later, she was shocked to discover that an hour and a half had lapsed since she'd started reading.

Finally, when it felt like her eyes wouldn't stay open any longer, she closed the book and walked to the kitchen, placing her mug in the dishwasher and turning it to start.

She dressed in her pajamas and set her phone charging across the room before climbing into bed. The minute the lights turned off, she felt her mind click back to the email. And this was why she should have left her phone on silent to begin with. It was also why she shouldn't have looked at the message in the first place.

Her mind jumped into gear as she considered who might have sent the email. Could it be someone she knew from before she moved to Key West? She wracked her brain, but the only person that came to mind readily was Uncle Sal.

She quickly pushed that thought away because he was

dead. For some reason, she'd been thinking about him the other day which is likely why he'd come up again. Was it someone related to him and his business? He'd helped many people in his days as a private investigator, but no one would associate her with him in that way.

Then again, she'd started helping him in her teens and on into her early twenties when she was on breaks from school. She hadn't been the one to crack any major leads, but she also hadn't been *inactive*. Uncle Sal had taught her so much, enough to get her out of a few difficult situations, as well as her recent interactions with those on the wrong side of the law.

But surely that couldn't play into the email. It had only come to mind because of the direction of her thoughts the other day at the beach. Yes, that had to be it.

Closing her eyes, Eva tried her best not to think of anything specifically. Instead, she pictured the ocean waves crashing to the shore over and over again. It was a technique she'd learned from a counselor in the months after her parent's death, and it had really helped with the horrific nightmares she'd suffered from after that tragedy.

And tonight, like it had when she'd started it all those years ago, it put her right to sleep.

3

SATURDAY MORNING DAWNED bright and early for Eva. Elena, the maid that Eva hired to clean the rooms and main areas of the bed-and-breakfast, was called to her other job which left Eva to Elena's work. It was something that didn't happen often, but Eva tried to be very understanding of the girl's other jobs.

Many times, Eva had considered adding another maid to the rotation for just such situations but then Elena would catch wind and beg her not to. It was more that she didn't want her hours cut, something Eva understood and wouldn't allow to happen. On occasion, she'd had to hire temporary help in the summertime when the guest turnover was too busy and even now she was considering it again.

It wasn't so much that she minded the cleaning, but she did like the idea of employing another person in need of work, and it would give her some flexibility. What if she wasn't able to fill in for Elena? They would be in a bind and that was never good.

Making up her mind, she added a to-do note to Benita's list. Benita Alverez was the housekeeper for the bed-and-breakfast. A title that barely scraped the surface of what the capable woman did. She usually got the weekends off, something Eva was happy to offer her, but her list on Monday would be slightly more than normal.

Eva finished cleaning the last room around eleven and took a late breakfast in the sunroom. The chef, Anton, had outdone himself with the Saturday breakfast and she was enjoying the last bites of a waffle when inspiration struck.

She was in the mood to take pictures.

Something she'd read in her photography book came back to her in that moment. The author suggested taking photos as often as possible when first starting out. His theory was that while the learning curve was quite extreme at the onset, the more a person took photos, the more they learned, and the easier photography would become for them.

She'd taken that to heart, but for the last few days, she'd not felt the tug of inspiration. Admittedly, she'd been a little frustrated with her lack of progress, and while her photo of the MMBC had turned out all right, she still didn't *love* the way it looked.

"Need anything else, Ms. Eva?"

She snapped out of her refection to meet Anton's gaze. He was a hulk of a man with deeply tanned skin and black hair. His fierce exterior was softened by a constant smile and the fact that he could out-cook anyone she knew.

"No, thank you. It was delicious."

"I'm going to head out then."

"You have a lovely Saturday."

"You do the same," he said before slipping from the bright and sunny room. The air-conditioning, along with the shade from palm trees, was crucial with all of the windows in the sunroom. Even still, it was slightly warmer in there than the rest of the bed-and-breakfast, but she didn't mind the warmth.

Even now, with a full stomach and quite a bit of work behind her from that morning, she was tempted to take a nap on the porch. But the thought of taking photos came back to her and she shoved to standing. No more putting off practice. She was going down to the beach because that's where she'd last gotten inspiration, and she thought maybe that would help now too.

Fifteen minutes later, the wind whipped her long skirt about her ankles, and she held onto her straw hat as her bare toes dug into the sand. She was glad she'd brought a large tote to keep her camera bag in because she quickly realized it was going to be impossible to keep her hat on during the photo taking. At least not if she wanted it to *stay* on her head.

Taking care not to smash the brim too much, she gently slipped the hat into her bag, tossed the strap over her shoulder, and headed toward the water. She'd kept her camera free in case she was struck by inspiration, and she was soon glad she had.

A beautiful sand dollar had washed ashore, nestled in the sand as if waiting for her to take its picture.

"You just hold on," she muttered to the sand dollar, smiling at the fact she was talking to a type of sea creature.

She adjusted her settings and snapped a few photos, happy to see she'd gotten it right. The sand dollar wasn't too washed out by the light sand around it. The detail was good as well. She was improving!

She moved on, leaving the sand dollar for another lucky beachcomber to find. Now she turned her lens on the vegetation edging the sand. It made a nice contrast to the light color of the beach, and she snapped a photo of it. This time when she checked the balance, she was sad to see she'd gotten the sand photographed correctly, but the tree line was much too dark. Overall, it was a terrible picture.

Sighing, she put her camera to her eye and scanned along to see what she wanted to take a photo of next. It was odd, viewing the world through the lens of a camera, but it did help her to stop thinking of *everything* she saw as a potential for a photo and instead to think of the landscape within the aspect of the viewfinder.

As she was swinging her camera toward the water again, she jolted back as a face appeared much too close. She yanked down the camera only to find that the face she'd seen was still yards away.

But it was a face she recognized.

"Detective Makos," she said as he walked up to her.

He wore khaki shorts and a white linen shirt opened several buttons down to reveal tanned olive skin. He had on dark sunglasses and carried canvas shoes by their heels in a relaxed manner. In fact, all of the usually stern detective looked relaxed.

"Please, it's Jerome. I'm off duty."

"I see that." She couldn't help the appreciative glance she gave him. She'd never seen him look this...normal.

"You seem surprised. I don't work all the time."

"Could have fooled me," she said, dropping her camera to her side with the strap over her shoulder.

"Oh come on," he said with a chuckle. "I have a life outside of the department."

She just looked at him.

He barked out a laugh. "Why, Ms. Stewart, dare I judge you of the same thing? What are you doing? Casing some place? Following someone you're taking photos of?"

Her jaw dropped open. "I'll have you know that I am not doing anything of the sort. I've taken up photography. As a hobby." She almost said an *innocent* hobby, but she didn't want him to think she needed to clarify.

"A hobby, huh?"

"Yes." She took a breath. She sounded defiant. "Yes, I have always wanted to study photography but never found the time, so I'm making time."

"That's nice," he said and sounded like he meant it.

"Unfortunately, I think I'm horrible at taking pictures," she admitted before she could stop herself.

Now he grinned. "You can't be that bad."

"Maybe not, but I don't tend to do things unless I can do them well. I'm contemplating giving up."

"Oh, come on." He held out his hand. "Here, let me see."

"See my photos? No way." She leaned to the side so he couldn't reach her camera.

"You're not going to let me look at them?"

"No."

He took a step toward her, the wind whipping his loose shirt about his torso even as her hair tried to escape the low knot she'd wrestled it into.

"I know a thing or two about photography. Let me help you."

She looked up into his green eyes that were almost the color of the water and felt something inside of her shift toward trusting him. Was she truly so stubborn that she wouldn't accept help?

"Oh fine. But don't judge me too harshly. I've only just begun." She lifted the camera strap off her shoulder and handed it over to him.

Jerome took the camera in his hands in a way that made her think he was no stranger to holding a digital camera. His fingers went right to the correct view button and soon he was scrolling through her photos.

When he came to the end, he looked up. "You're doing really well."

Her brow furrowed. "But?"

His lips parted to show white teeth. "You just need to line up your shutter speed and aperture with your conditions."

He went on to give her some very practical tips, having her apply them to where they were now and the different tableaus she could photograph from just that one spot.

With his expert instruction, she started to see progress in her photos. "This is amazing!" Eva said after taking another shot of the tree line, rich with lush vegetation. It didn't take her long to get the exposure balance correct.

"You're doing great. You're a very quick study."

"Thank you," she said, taking in a deep breath of satisfaction. "It's a lot to understand, but it helps to see it in action, you know?"

"I do."

He'd turned to look out at the water, hands in his pockets. He was the picture of a peaceful man. "Why do you know so much about photography?"

The corner of his mouth turned, but she wasn't graced with a full smile since his eyes stayed on the water. "I spent some time in college as a photography minor. At first, I was thinking I would go into it full-time, but my dad didn't like that idea. So, I switched to forensics. As you know, photography plays a big role in that."

"But?" She pressed when he hesitated.

"I was *encouraged* to pursue 'higher' things."

"Like becoming a detective."

"Yeah." He sounded resigned but not exactly unhappy. "It's how things worked out so I can't complain. I still get to take photos occasionally, and it's generally of things I enjoy. I count that as a bonus."

She didn't say anything, mostly because she wasn't sure what to say. He'd never spoken so openly about himself before, and she thought that perhaps that had to do with the fact that every other time they'd talked, he'd been working a case.

If she was forced to admit it, she would say she liked this relaxed, non-working version of Jerome better, though she wasn't sure that sounded right in her mind.

Instead, she said, "I can understand a little of what it's like to have expectations on you."

"Yeah?" He angled a glance over at her.

"Yes. I actually wanted to be a private investigator when I grew up."

She said the admission while looking out at the ocean, not wanting to see the inevitable laughter he'd have at that statement. She knew he'd already looked into her background and had made the connection between her and her Uncle Sal, but this was different. She was freely talking to him about her past.

"What stopped you?"

The lack of humor in his words caused her to sneak a peek at him, but he looked the same, staring out at the endless waves.

"My father was a high-priced lawyer and my mother was a socialite from old money. They had expectations for me, so I studied business and international relations."

"Quite the tradeoff."

"Hardly," she admitted. "I enjoyed it. I thought I might work for a foreign embassy which my parents would have loved but..." She trailed off.

"But?"

"I joined the company my mother's family ran. I worked within the international branches of the business and learned a lot, but I came home exhausted every day. I never felt like I accomplished much.

"But you're down here now."

"We used to come down here for vacations. I don't know why. For some reason my father liked the warm climate and the feeling. Something about him coming here as a kid. When my parents died…" She paused and swallowed. Jerome already knew the details because he'd looked into her background, but it was still hard to talk about. "Well, I decided to move down here. I've always loved the idea of a bed-and-breakfast. My mother and I went to so many while my father was busy with work. Our little trips, as she'd call them. So, I took all that information, purchased the Key's house and transitioned it to suit my needs."

"And you've been here ever since."

"I have."

"You like it?"

"I do. But what about you? This is a far cry from New York."

He grinned. "Exactly."

"What does that mean?" The wind had died down, so she pulled her hat on to give her face and shoulders shade.

"It means that I wanted the slower pace. It's not typical to go from a place like New York to place like Key West while still on the job, but it wasn't a decision I made lightly. I enjoy the pace of life here. The people. The beach." He gestured toward the water. "I'm going to get a boat, and I'm going to work here until I retire. At least that's the plan."

She smiled. It sounded like a pretty good plan to her.

The sun moved lower in the sky, but they stood there

for a little while longer, enjoying the warmth of the sun, the cool light breeze, and the easy, companionable silence.

Finally, he turned to her, "Good luck with your photography. If you need any more pointers, let me know."

She wanted to ask him to get dinner with her, but something about that felt too intimate. They had worked two cases together—though 'worked together' sounded too willing on his part if she were to be honest. But she wanted to get him to relax around her. Her last attempt at that had been when she'd invited him to the MMBC and that had certainly failed—he'd come once never to come again.

If he couldn't manage that, a dinner with a new friend might also be out of the question. And for reasons Eva wasn't keen on digging into, that made her sad.

"I will. Good to see you, Jerome."

"And you."

He dipped his head once in goodbye and walked off down the sandy beach. She watched him go for a few minutes before snapping a quick photo of his retreating form.

***

"HELLO?" Eva picked up her phone, one hand holding her pan above the stove so as not to overheat the sauce she was making.

"Hey Eva, it's Vicky."

"Oh hello," she said, shifting the phone to position it

between her shoulder and ear so she could still stir the sauce. "What are you—Oops!" She almost dropped the phone but managed to catch it before it fell.

"Sounds like I caught you at a bad time."

"Sorry." Eva chuckled. She pulled the pan to the back of the stove and turned off the burner. "I'm just making dinner. What's up?"

"I was wondering if you might want to go with me to the Great White Heron National Wildlife Refuge tomorrow."

"The Great White—what?"

Vicky laughed. "I know—long name, right? I was doing some research on outdoor places near Key West and saw an advertisement about this place. It's amazing and a refuge for the Great White Heron. I hear it's perfect for landscape photographers."

Eva's eyebrows rose. "Is that a hint to stop taking pictures of people?"

"Not at all," Vicky rushed to say. "I just...thought you might like a chance to photograph someplace different than what you're used to, and I'd love to see the refuge."

For some reason Eva felt like Vicky wasn't telling her the whole story.

"Okay, Vicky. Spill the beans. What are you keeping from me? Are there alligators everywhere or something?"

"No," Vicky laughed. "Nothing like that but...I didn't get the idea myself."

Eva tried to puzzle through what that meant. "Huh?"

"I may have heard from a reliable source that you're a good nature photographer and I thought that—"

"Wait. Who told you that?" Eva thought over what her friend had said but didn't need to wait for confirmation. "Jerome."

"Busted." Vicky didn't sound sorry at all. "He said he'd seen some of the photos you were taking and that you had a good eye for landscape and nature. The Wildlife Refuge was my idea though. I keep seeing advertisements for it online and every place I go, it seems. They need the funding, so I'm game to help."

Eva couldn't help the small smile that tugged the corners of her lips skyward. While Jerome hadn't said anything when they were talking, it was interesting to note that he had considered her nature photos better than her other ones. Granted, she wasn't exactly *good* at any of them really, but it was kind of him to suggest a nature excursion to Vicky.

"Well, I think that sounds like a lovely idea. I'd be happy to go with you and I'd love to support the refuge as well."

As soon as the words were out, Eva thought back to the previous case she'd solved where she'd found herself investing heavily in another wildlife refuge around Key West. It seemed it was her year to support nature, but she didn't mind one bit.

"Oh good!" Vicky sounded excited. "I haven't told many people this because they always look at me strangely, but I just love birds."

Eva laughed. "You do realize I own a parrot, don't you?"

Vicky snort-chuckled. "You know, I hadn't made that

connection. Weird. Maybe I'm too used to working with dead people."

It was Eva's turn to laugh. "Maybe."

"So, tomorrow, ten at my place? We can catch a taxi boat out to the refuge."

"Sounds perfect."

"See you tomorrow."

"Tomorrow then."

As Eva hung up, she felt the tingle of anticipation at the thought of a small adventure with her friend, and she was excited at the opportunity to take more photos. Perhaps she'd even show some of her better ones to Jerome for his expert opinion.

Moments later her stomach growled, and her mind quickly turned back to dinner. She finished pulling together the sauce and noodles, topping the dish with herb-encrusted baked chicken.

As she sat down at the table, her eye went to her photography gear occupying less than half the bench seat in front of the large bay window that overlooked the pool. She usually kept the curtains closed during the busiest guest seasons, but she'd left the slatted blinds open tonight. The peaceful surface of the pool with lights reflecting back into the night made her heart soar.

Everything felt good. Right. As if she were finally settling into the busy season. She liked the feeling of not being in a rush and being able to enjoy each season of life.

For some reason, her thoughts of late had been occupied with the past. The memory of Uncle Sal on the beach, as well as the strange email that made her think of him. It was all clouding her judgment, making her think more about the past as opposed to the future.

Thankfully, tomorrow would be another chance for her to enjoy the present with her good friend, and she'd also get to play around with her new obsession of photography. It was certainly something to look forward to.

4

"This refuge was established in 1938…" their tour guide was saying.

"It says here the demand for feathers in the early 1900s nearly made the herons extinct!" Vicky whispered, holding up the pamphlet they'd gotten at the visitor center.

"Shhh," Eva said as the guide looked at Vicky. Her nose was still stuck in the foldout pamphlet.

"Sorry," she said, peering above the large paper.

The guide continued down the path, but Eva stayed back giving Vicky time to refold her pamphlet.

"Our guide is likely telling us everything in that," Eva said, looking amused.

"I've always been a better reader than an audial learner," Vicky said with an apologetic smile.

They walked down the path to catch up with their group just as the guide stopped them at another vantage point. Eva pulled out her camera and started taking shots as the man spoke.

"We have almost two hundred thousand acres free for birds and wildlife of all kinds here in the backcountry."

Eva had heard the term backcountry applied to the wilderness areas in Florida but had never truly been to anything categorized as that. She was now feeling like that had been a mistake. The water was a striking turquoise blue, and it was so clear you could see straight to the bottom in the shallow areas.

Out on the water, she observed people in kayaks and fishing boats. It seemed everyone was enjoying the beautiful day. She couldn't help noticing there were no jet skis, which was a nice reprieve from the usually busy waters closer to Key West.

In a word, the refuge was restful and beautiful. Everything she wanted in a Sunday adventure with Vicky. She was also getting some great shots—in her humble opinion—and was so glad she'd brought along a borrowed telephoto lens to get close-up shots of some of the birds. Granted, with the extended distance her camera had, she hadn't accounted for the sheer weight of the lens. At the start of the day, it had felt like five easy pounds, but now it felt closer to twenty.

"Here," Vicky said, handing her the water bottle from the side pouch on Eva's backpack. "You look thirsty."

Eva took it gratefully and considered taking the large lens off to stow in her backpack. She had a few smaller lenses that would still do a good job, they just wouldn't get her as close.

"Okay folks, if you'll follow me this way, we'll wrap up our tour," the guide said.

As they walked, Eva decided once they had some autonomy from the group, she'd take a few more zoomed-in shots and then put the bulky lens away. She followed the group to a shaded area. While the relief from the sun felt nice, the heat and humidity only worsened as they walked away from the open water.

"Whew, it is *hot*," Vicky observed.

"Very," Eva agreed.

"Thanks so much for your cooperation," the guide said. "You have several options for self-guided tours. They're located on the back of your pamphlet." He distinctly gave Vicky a look, and Eva nearly laughed out loud before she stopped herself.

Someone at the front asked a question and everyone chucked, but Eva hadn't caught it. Instead, she was looking around the circular area and caught sight of several trail entrances.

"Lastly," the guide said, drawing her attention back, "I'll point out a few options for trails. To my right..." He pointed with two fingers. "We've got the Great White Heron trail. Yes, you're almost guaranteed to see at least one Great White Heron while on this trail, but there's no money-back guarantee, folks."

More laughter. The guide was good at his job, and she caught sight of where the Great White Heron trail led them through a more forested area.

"Then directly behind you, branching off of the trail

we just came on, is the Seaside Trail, and to your right is the Snapper Trail."

He made a joke about the name, but it was Eva's turn to be engrossed by the pamphlet. "I think we should try the Seaside Trail."

"I don't know if I'm going to make it," Vicky said, and Eva looked up to see her waving her pamphlet in front of her like a fan.

"I think it'll be better since it looks open on one side to the water. There's bound to be a breeze, whereas the Great White Heron trail is more wooded. That sounds hotter."

"Whatever your photographer's eye wants," Vicky said with a laugh as the group dispersed.

"Come on, Chad," a woman said, tugging on the hand of a young boy. "We're going to take the Seaside Trail."

"Can't we go back?" the little boy asked.

"No, sweetie. I told your father we'd get pictures of a Great White Heron, and they're best seen on the water trail." The mother pointed to the same trail Eva was looking at taking.

The little boy sighed dramatically, and then followed his mother just as Eva and Vicky headed in the same direction of the trail. They were coming near the entrance when a man nearly knocked Vicky over on his way to the trail entrance.

"Ouch," Vicky said, latching onto her arm where his elbow had connected.

"Sorry," he said gruffly, pulling down the sides of his

fisherman's cap. He was tall and wore a black shirt with olive-green cargo pants. He had on heavy boots that looked well-worn.

Vicky gave Eva a look that said, *Really?* But they both shook off the rude interaction and took the trail behind the mother and young boy who were already several yards ahead of them. The man was beyond that, walking at a quick pace.

Where could someone be going to in such a rush?

When the trail opened up to the ocean on one side and lush greens on the other, Vicky tossed her arms out. "Much better," she said, enjoying the stiff breeze.

"I agree," Eva said, hefting the heavy lens up. It was almost time for her to put it away, but first she wanted to take advantage of the dock for viewing.

They took to the wooden planks, water lapping at the base. Eva started from one side of the island and took photos moving all along the coast until she was facing the other way. Her arms were growing tired, so she let them rest on the railing, sighting her next shot when something caught her attention.

Down the shoreline, there was movement. Something —or was it a person?—was running through the trees. Were they running to something or away? She swung the camera up the coastline and froze when she saw the tall man who had nearly knocked Vicky over. He stood still now, but from her vantage point she could see booted feet on the ground. Feet that weren't moving.

"Uh, Vicky," Eva tried to zoom in, but she was at the

max capacity of the lens. "I think someone needs help. Down the beach."

Vicky looked where Eva was pointing but without the aid of the camera, it was nearly impossible to see.

"We should go," she said, slipping into medical examiner mode.

They rushed back the way they'd come and then took to running up the beach. It wasn't easy due to lose rocks and lack of a good path, but as they rounded the corner, they met the same man rushing their way. He looked pale and startled to see them.

"I—help," was all he could manage, thrusting a finger behind him.

"I'm a doctor," Vicky said, and rushed past him.

Eva followed her friend but came to a sudden stop at Vicky's side at the sight they discovered.

A woman lay sprawled on her back, eyes blank and staring heavenward with no sign of life in them.

"I KNOW this isn't ideal, folks, but we need to wait until the proper authorities arrive."

The Fish and Wildlife Federal Officer had introduced himself as Paul Hart as he pulled off a pair of leather gloves and shoved them into his back pocket. He was in his early fifties with unruly salt and pepper hair. His skin was tanned to a dark tone, likely from hours in the sun.

He was sweating heavily, and she couldn't blame him.

Despite the air-conditioned visitor center they were all sitting in, it was clear that Paul Hart had never trained for something like discovering a dead body on a wildlife refuge.

Outside, Eva could see Vicky pacing back and forth on the phone, likely discussing with her office what they would need. Being that Key West was surrounded by islands, there was no doubt that the police had several boats at their convenience, but she also had a feeling it wasn't every day they had to water-transport a dead body that might be part of a murder investigation.

While Eva hadn't gone close to the body, she'd seen enough of the markings on the woman's neck to assume it hadn't been accidental. Of course, that was a determination the police would have to make.

But why did a dead body have to show up when she was relaxing? It felt selfish to think such a thing, especially in the face of the poor woman who had died, but it was disconcerting, nonetheless.

Eva turned back to the room and observed those who had shown up. The guide from before was trying to console another young woman who Eva had seen running the gift shop when they first arrived. They looked to be good friends, and she could only imagine the tragedy of it all.

Two small families took up the benches on the opposite side of the center. Eva also noticed the mother and young boy she'd seen earlier. The mom was trying her best to keep the boy occupied while covertly dabbing at her eyes when he wasn't looking.

Next to them, on her phone, was a thin blonde woman next to a hulking man. She wore tan cargo shorts, a white tank top, hiking boots, and had a floppy she was twisting around in her hand. Th man wore dark pants that looked to be a type of light hiking material and a loose-fitting dark shirt that showed off muscular arms. He wore no hat, only sunglasses that rested backward against his neck. He looked to be South American or perhaps Cuban.

Across from them, the man they'd run into earlier sat alone staring out the window. He looked traumatized, but Eva couldn't blame him. She'd unfortunately seen more dead bodies within the year than she would like to admit, and while it didn't get easier, it did start to become something a person adjusted to. It was the only way that Vicky could do her job, Eva surmised.

Paul checked his phone, and then put it back in the hip holster in front of the gun he wore.

"Any news?" Eva asked.

"The police are minutes away. Good thing too. Can you tell I don't have a clue what I'm doing?" He tried to smile, but the action fell flat. He looked stunned. "I've got a daughter close in age to that...the woman." He swallowed and wiped a hand over his mouth.

"It's a shame," Eva said, unsure what else to say.

"It is." The haunted look returned, and he turned his gaze to the window.

Poor man, Eva thought. He was just doing his job, thinking the biggest thing he had to worry about was a visitor doing something to hurt the wildlife, and yet here was a dead body.

"Ah," he said, pointing his head toward the front dock where they'd been dropped off by their water taxi. "That'll be them."

He took in a fortifying breath and squared his shoulders before turning to the room. "Folks, just stay put. I'm going to bring the police in, and they'll likely have questions for you. When they're done, you can get on your way home."

"But why do we have to stay?" one father asked. He had a protective arm around his son. "We didn't do anything."

"Not saying you did," Paul said. "Just stay put, all right? Procedure and all." He tried to smile again, but it never made it to his eyes.

When Eva turned, she caught sight of Jerome stepping off the boat and making his way toward them. His hair wasn't long, and yet it whipped about in the wind along with his police windbreaker. He wore a scowl that she was beginning to call his 'crime face'.

She watched as he met Vicky outside the visitor center and then turned to greet Paul with a firm handshake. The men spoke for several minutes, and then Jerome made his way inside. He pulled off his sunglasses as he stepped through the front door and immediately his gaze flew to her.

"This wasn't what I had in mind when I suggested Vicky take you out to photograph nature."

She lifted one shoulder. "I wouldn't say it's what I had in mind either."

He huffed a breath, then faced the room. "Hello everyone. I'm Detective Makos with the Key West PD. We'll be conducting the investigation, and we'll try our best to get you back home as soon as possible. My officers will be coming in shortly to take your statements if you'll just wait for them."

He nodded once, and when no one spoke up, he made his way to Eva. "But really, you had to pick the *one* place there was a dead body?" He whispered the last part, sending a look at a young girl between her parents. She was obviously occupied with the small toys the gift shop clerk had brought out for her, but Eva was happy to see Jerome was sensitive to the situation.

"I don't know what to tell you other than Vicky likely saw the advertisements all over town like the rest of this group."

"You don't know that's why they're here," Jerome said, laughing at her audacity.

"The couple there, with the girl? They have an advertisement that comes with a coupon for free child access—it's in the mother's backpack. And..." Eva tilted her head toward the man at the window. "I saw he had one sticking out of his back pocket earlier. But I suppose you're right about not all of them coming because of that. I'm pretty sure the young woman over there and her hulk aren't here because of a flier."

Jerome covertly assessed them as well and shrugged. "I guess we'll find out. I'll need to have someone take your statement."

"Naturally." She smiled back at him, and he turned to

go, but then he paused, looking back at her. "Did you get any good shots?"

She chuckled softly so as not to draw attention. "That remains to be seen, but I'll let you know."

He nodded and left the visitor center in a rush of humid wind.

5

EVA GAVE her statement to an officer and then waited while Vicky and Jerome spoke outside. She assumed from their body language that he was explaining what he needed from her, and she was agreeing since there was a lot of nodding going on. Finally, she walked off in the direction of where the body was, followed by several lab techs, while he turned back to the visitor center.

Eva hung back as Jerome made a beeline toward the grumpy man who still sat alone. While she didn't usually allow herself to be nosy, she angled up as close as she dared as Jerome began to question the man. Why had he been in such a rush to go down the path earlier, and then why had *he* been the only one they saw near the body?

"You're uh…" Jerome looked at a notepad. "Darnell Forrester?"

"Yeah," the man said. He had an abrupt manner that Eva found out of place while being questioned by the police.

"And you found the body?"

"Well, yeah. After that other guy."

"Guy?"

Eva couldn't help it. She looked over at the man—Darnell—as he stared back at Jerome.

"What guy?" Jerome asked.

"I was…out walking, you know. It's a nature preserve, and I was enjoying the flora and fauna. Anyway, I came upon this clearing and saw…" He swallowed, taking moment to compose himself. "I saw this guy leaning over the…the body."

"Can you describe him to me?"

"Sure." The man's eyes turned toward the ceiling in recall. "Tallish, about my height which is six feet two inches. Had reddish-blond hair, really wild-looking and not combed. He was kind of round around the middle and wearing, I don't know…jeans and a black t-shirt I think."

Jerome was scribbling furiously. "Had you ever seen him before?"

"No."

"Did you recognize the body?"

"Uh, no. Not really." Darnell looked away again, looking like he might be sick.

Jerome wrote some more. "And why were you here today?"

"The, uh, advertisement. In the paper."

Whether it was conscious or subconscious, Jerome's gaze turned toward Eva, and she was caught listening in, though he didn't seem to mind.

"Officer McCulley is going to take down the rest of your details, all right?"

"Sure. Yeah."

Jerome flipped his notebook closed, tucked it into his coat pocket, and turned back to Eva. "Eavesdropping, Ms. Stewart?"

She was caught red-handed, and yet if she was reading Jerome correctly, he didn't seem mad.

"Not exactly." It was partly true.

"Come on. Let's go find Vicky."

She blinked, shocked by his offer, but rushed to follow after him. Her camera gear was weighing down her shoulders, biting in with the heavy straps, but she didn't care. As if sensing her thoughts, Jerome paused outside the door and looked at the gear she was holding.

"Want to stow your camera in the boat?"

"That would be great," she admitted. He had a tech take it back to the PD's boat and then beckoned her down the path.

"So, you were taking photos in that direction." He pointed toward where the body had been found. "And that's when you saw Darnell back there—right after he'd just found the body."

This conversational side of Jerome was sending her for a loop, and she wasn't sure if she'd proven herself in the last case or if it was just a good day, but she wasn't about to question it.

"Yes, I was taking photos over there. And now that you mention it, it did look like someone was running through the trees. I believe there's a path there—the Great White Heron path."

"I'll get someone to check it out. Did you see details of the person running away?"

"Sadly, no. It's pretty heavily forested, and I wasn't sure at first if it was human or animal. But the movement was big enough to catch my attention. Then I looked more closely and came across Mr. Forrester standing there. He looked…shocked."

"I'll say." Jerome shook his head as they rounded the same bend.

Eva knew the crime scene was just a few yards ahead, and she took a deep breath to mentally prepare herself.

Jerome paused. "I'm sorry. I didn't even ask you if you were okay coming back here."

She faced him, the honesty in her gaze no doubt telling him she wasn't ready, but she wouldn't admit that. Where this stubbornness was coming from, she wasn't exactly sure, but it reminded her of Uncle Sal. History coming back up once again.

"I'll be fine."

He stared at her for a moment longer, as if to gauge her honesty, but then he turned and forged ahead.

Soon she saw Vicky knelt next to the woman's body as a photographer orbited around them taking shots from all angles.

Immediately, Eva noticed several things, most of them nowhere near the body because she couldn't bring herself to look for very long. For one thing, there was quite a bit of soft dirt and wet dirt closer to the water. While the crime scene techs wore booties so as not to disturb the area, and she and Jerome stood on the stones near the water's edge, it was clear there were at least three, possibly four, sets of shoe prints. Two, maybe three, that looked similar in size, and there was one that looked smaller.

A quick glance at the dead woman's feet showed a sole that would match the smaller size and tread. Perhaps Darnell had been telling the truth about the other man which her visual would corroborate. If there were four sets though, who was responsible for the fourth pair?

Finally, she noticed that they had walked past a sign stating no entry. She hadn't noticed it when she and Vicky had been coming to see what was going on—something easily overlooked when more important things are at hand. But this time she had clearly stepped past the sign, which itself didn't look all too permanent.

She filed the information away in the back of her mind and looked to the edges of the crime scene area. There were several forensics team members who likely worked with Vicky on most cases. They filled the area looking for clues. They seemed to have moved from the west side to the east, but as Eva looked to the west, she saw something that was not native to the area.

"Um, Jerome?" He finished a comment to a tech before meeting her gaze.

"Yeah?"

"I think I see something odd over there. I don't think it's plant matter."

He followed where she was pointing, but perhaps due

to the angle of where he stood, he couldn't see it. Frowning, he shifted past her. Being careful to keep to the solid ground and away from any prints, he made his way around the area to where she pointed, kneeling down.

"Hey, can I get a number and a photographer over here?"

"What is it?" Eva said, unable to keep the curiosity from her voice.

"Looks like…" He leaned down, then back. "A strap of some kind."

The booted photographer made her way over, placed a yellow sign with a number on it next to the item, and took several photos. When she nodded that she was finished, Jerome took a pen from his pocket and picked up the strap. It was around two and a half feet in length and had a silver clasp at one end.

Eva squinted to see. It was difficult since she was almost ten feet away, but then her eyes moved to the woman's body. While it was hard to tell, she thought she caught faint lines on the victim's neck.

"Is it a camera strap?" Eva thought it looked similar to hers.

"Looks like it. She may have been strangled with it," Jerome said, looking in the same direction.

Eva shivered at the thought.

"But we'll have to wait for the autopsy, right Vicky?" he said with a half-smile.

"Right." She was so focused on her examination, she didn't even look up. And perhaps it was best not to have any outside sources at this point. Eva wasn't sure.

"Good eye," Jerome said, coming back to stand next to Eva. "How'd you see that?"

"Not sure, actually. I just knew it didn't belong with the brush in this area.

"I'm surprised the techs didn't catch it. They likely would have on their second walk through, but I'm glad to have it now."

She nodded just as Vicky stood.

"I think that's all I'll get from here. I'll need the body transported to my lab for the rest of the examination."

"You got it." Jerome helped her slip out of the blue cloth booties she'd pulled over her hiking shoes. "You ladies need a ride back?"

"Please," Vicky said.

Eva nodded as well.

"I'll have them take you across to the parking lot since we'll be here for a while longer. Don't leave town," he said to Eva who smiled.

"Noted," she said with a smile.

Then they turned to leave, but Jerome called out to her. "Really though, thanks for catching the strap."

"Of course," Eva said.

At that moment, she realized that the way Jerome looked at her did funny things to twist her stomach. If it hadn't been for the dead body just behind him, she might have said something flirty, but death had a special way of stopping thoughts like that.

"I CAN'T BELIEVE this happened on a day that was supposed to be filled with relaxing photography opportunities." Vicky sat shoulder to shoulder with Eva on the police department's boat as it cut effortlessly through the water back to the parking area. "I mean, of all the things…we come across a dead body?"

"It certainly wasn't what I'd envisioned," Eva said, her thoughts going back to what she'd seen before the body had been found. "Did you recognize the woman? The, uh, victim?"

Vicky shook her head. "I didn't see her on the tour. Did you?"

"I was trying to recall if I had," Eva said, her eyes taking in the vibrant blue water surrounding them. "But I think I might have seen her in the gift shop before the tour started. You went to the restroom, and I'm fairly certain it was her. But…I didn't get a great look at her at the scene."

"That's a good thing, Vicky said, gently squeezing Eva's knee. "I'm glad you're not as comfortable with the deceased as I am."

"Honestly, I'm glad for that as well. But I keep thinking about what she must have gone through."

"It's best if you don't think of it."

"But the *how* could inform the *why*, isn't that true?"

Vicky looked over at Eva, evaluating her.

"What?" Eva said.

"You're doing it again." Vicky's lips twisted into a chagrined smile. "You're trying to solve this mystery."

Eva shrugged. "Not so much solve as to make sense of it. It doesn't follow that, on an island like we were just on, someone could get away with murder like that. Someone we saw was probably the killer."

Vicky's eyes went wide. "I'm used to dealing with the aftermath of murder, not murderers themselves. Do you think we're in danger?" She looked to the young police officer driving the boat as if he might need to step in an save them at any minute.

"I doubt that we are," Eva said, offering her friend a comforting smile. Then Eva straightened.

"What?" Vicky asked, looking worried.

"Unless she was killed before the island opened up to visitors."

Vicky frowned. "Based on my findings, I'd say she was killed not too long before we got to her."

"I'd thought as much." Eva let out a sigh. "Still, there isn't an infinite number of suspects so that's good."

"True. But Eva..." Vicky turned to look back at the island shrinking in the distance. "Why would someone kill her like that? I mean, with a limited number of people on the island, the killer would have known that they'd probably be found and—"

"Not exactly," Eva said, remembering the sign she'd seen. "I think someone might have been counting on her not being found immediately. Either that or they were interrupted while trying to dispose of the body."

Vicky shivered. "I'm a medical examiner and that still creeps me out."

"Good," Eva said, squeezing her friend's hand. "That will keep you on your toes."

"You just said we weren't in danger." Vicky speared her with a look.

"Oh, you know what I mean."

Eva turned to look out at the water again. They were nearing the dock where their water taxi had taken off from that morning. Eva had ridden with Vicky to the dock, and they'd be able to return to the ME's car quickly. But her mind was more preoccupied about the limited pool of suspects Jerome was working with.

She tried to take stock from what she remembered. There was the Federal Fish and Wildlife officer, Paul Hart, who was responsible for handing the case over to Jerome. There were also the two other workers on the island—the guide and the gift shop worker.

Then there was Darnell who'd found the woman. He said he saw a mysterious man running away from the body, but that person never showed up in the visitor center.

There was Lilly and Tim—she'd overheard the names of the hiking couple—in addition to the mother and son. She'd also seen a couple other families with children, and of course, she was there with Vicky.

Not a lot of likely suspects really. Many had acted strangely, but one never knew how someone might react to finding a dead body. There was certainly no right way to do so.

"You're investigating," Vicky said, leaning close to Eva. "I can see it in that focused stare."

Eva rolled her eyes and shrugged. "We'll have to check the boat logs, but if it's true that only our taxi and a few before it, took passengers to the island, then it's very possible the killer was there with us. Unless they had their own boat, but that's unlikely since there's only one dock. It's simply a problem of figuring out who had motive and opportunity."

"Simple," Vicky said, picking up her backpack from the deck of the boat as it pulled up next to the dock. "But I need you to promise me that you'll be careful."

"Careful? I'm always careful."

Vicky speared her with a look. "I seem to remember you walking yourself into quite a few troublesome situations in the past, Miss Stewart. I don't want this to be yet another one of those."

"What if I promise to bring in the club on this?"

Vicky ignored her question for a moment as she stepped onto the dock with the help of an officer. "Thanks again, Stephen."

When they were several yards away, she rounded on Eva. "Oh honey, you know I won't let you solve this on your own. I've already sent out the text. We're meeting tonight."

Eva tossed her head back and laughed at the boldness of her friend. She should have expected it, but Vicky was good at misdirection.

"Deal. Have them meet at my place, and I'll make pizza."

"Willard will be pleased," Vicky said, pulling out her phone.

They reached her car and slid inside. She set the engine roaring to life, and they took off toward the bed-and-breakfast. Eva had a meeting to prepare for and a murder to solve.

6

THE SUMMER BEFORE, Eva had insisted that Ruben connect her with a mason to build a pizza oven in the bed-and-breakfast's backyard. There was a small corner just to the right of her cottage, and she'd thought it would be perfect for a small-scale oven. The man had outdone himself, and it had come in handy for all sorts of parties.

Tonight, the pizza oven would be put to good use when her friends showed up and made their own personal pizzas. She was currently in the kitchen fixing toppings and doing her best to clean as she went, knowing that Anton would not want to start his day with a messy kitchen.

The dough was already rising, and she'd started a few small logs which she would add to when it got closer to the club's arrival. Things we're looking good, and she was getting anxious to toss out the information to her friends to see their unique ideas on the matter of a murder on the wildlife refuge island.

Her friends—vast readers as they were—always had good insight into crimes, fictional or not, and Eva felt this one had the potential to baffle even the best of sleuths.

The bed-and-breakfast phone rang, and she dusted her hands free of flour before answering. "Hello?"

"Eva?"

"Yes. Who is this?"

"Jerome."

"I didn't recognize your voice," she said, leaning up against the counter cluttered with bowls of cheese, pepperoni, sausage, olives, onions, and more.

"Still out at the island. I tried your cell but got no answer."

"Oh." She pulled her phone from her pocket and saw his missed calls. "It was on silent. Sorry about that."

"No matter. I just wanted to let you know that we're fairly certain we know who the murderer is. I…I didn't want you to worry."

Her eyebrows rose. "So soon?"

"We're not done running everyone's backgrounds, but we did find out a few interesting things. One of which led us to the suspect in question. The man you and Darnell saw running from the scene."

"Are you sure?"

"Fairly certain."

Here Jerome hesitated and Eva felt she knew why. He'd called as a courtesy. To let her know she had no cause for alarm—not that she was worried—but it was clear now that he was telling her information about an open investigation.

"Thanks for letting me know," she began, but he kept going without acknowledging the out she'd offered.

"Logs at a private charger seem to indicate a man named Casey Ferrington took a boat out. He's got a rap sheet for drugs and spent some time in prison on an aggravated assault charge. He's not a nice guy, and it's our assumption that he was on the island looking for money for his next fix."

"But you haven't found him yet?"

"No, not yet, but it's only a matter of time. The warrant for his arrest ensures he won't get far."

"That is good news," she said. But she wasn't sure she believed it would be that easy.

While she was thankful he'd called to let her in the loop, she wasn't certain he had the right man. She couldn't put her finger on it, but something seemed…off.

"I just wanted you to know. To ease your mind." The caring in his words struck a chord in her.

"Thank you, Jerome. That is very kind of you." She could tell he wasn't sure what to say so she gave him an out. "I've got to get going—pizza oven is almost ready."

"Sounds like fun."

"Just having a little get together."

"Well, enjoy your night."

"I will. And Jerome…" She hesitated only a moment. "I hope you're not just stopping at the easy option."

His full laugh startled her. "Always the sleuth, eh Eva?"

She shrugged even though she knew he couldn't see her actions.

"I won't. Promise. Now go enjoy that pizza."

He hung up and she held the receiver a few more seconds before returning it to the holder. She didn't want him to think that she believed he was incompetent. From a police perspective, it would make sense that the man with the criminal record, and the man found fleeing the scene, *would* be the likely murderer, but it was a long way to go from assaulting someone to killing someone.

"But he knows that," she said to the kitchen.

Shaking her head, she covered the bowls of toppings and sauce, then went back to check on the pizza oven. Her friends would be arriving in a few minutes, and hopefully, Vicky would be able to make it as well despite the need to be working on the autopsy.

When Vicky had dropped Eva off, she'd made it clear she would come if she could get away for a dinner break. She'd share what she could, but she had no promises.

Eva didn't ever want to make her friend feel like she needed to share more than she ought to, but Vicky seemed to know that was the case. It was strange though because even Jerome seemed to be bending rules when it came to her now. Perhaps she'd proved herself in the last few cases they'd somewhat worked together.

Either way, she and the club would do their best to add a few more questions and possible parties to the board of suspects in the hopes that they could be of assistance to Jerome—even if he would insist he didn't need the help.

"This is delicious," Willard said, licking his fingers free of the red sauce and cheese dripping from his second pizza.

"Bonnie's going to kill *me* for letting you make two pizzas," Eva said, with a laugh.

"We did an extra-long walk today, it'll be fine." He winked and Eva was fairly certain it *wouldn't* be okay, but she'd let him tell his health-conscious wife.

"What a fun idea though," Kay said, perched on the teak lawn furniture. She wore a tank top that had little doggie bones all over it and flashed a smile at Pete as he and Elijah debated the latest thriller movie they'd both watched recently. "I love that you have a pizza oven! I want to get Pete to build us one, but he refuses. Says it'll take up too much space."

"You've got the space in the backyard," Geraldine said, from her seat on the recliner. She wore a long, flowy white dress and bright pink sandals that matched her bright pink headband.

"That's what I said, but he won't do it."

"Well, you're welcome to come over here any time for pizza," Eva said, finishing off the last piece of her pepperoni, black olive, and mushroom pizza.

"We'll take you up on that," Pete said, joining their conversation.

"What did I miss?" Elijah said after tossing his plate in the trash.

"Pizza," Geraldine said. "It's all about the pizza."

"Then let's make it all about the murder," Pete said.

All eyes turned to him.

"I'm sorry, was that my husband?" Kay feigned shock.

"What's gotten into you?" Willard asked.

"What do you mean?" Pete replied.

"It's always been 'when can we talk about books?'" Elijah pointed out.

Pete shrugged. "True, but this case sounds fascinating. I mean, an island only accessible by boat? A mysterious woman found dead? A limited number of people who could be the culprit? Sounds like a murder mystery waiting to happen."

"Except that it's real life," Kay gently pointed out.

"Right. Right. Except for that." Pete looked sheepish.

"I did invite you all over to discuss this," Eva said. "Maybe now is as good a time as any to start."

"But what about dessert?" Willard asked.

Everyone laughed, and after assuring Willard she had that covered as well, Eva directed them all to the porch and the private section set apart from guest access. She excused herself and got the wheeled cart with coffee and hot water for tea. She also added a plate of key lime bars for dessert.

By the time she was wheeling it out to the porch spot, Vicky had arrived. Elijah had made her a pizza per Eva's specifications, and Vicky was digging in like she hadn't eaten in days.

"Worked up the appetite, I see," Eva said just as Willard made a beeline for the desserts. "Only one," she warned him with a stern look.

He was smart enough to look sheepish, but she kept an eye on him anyway, making sure he only took one treat with his cup of coffee. Everyone else took their desserts and drinks to their seats, and then all eyes turned to Eva and Vicky.

She started off by telling them exactly what had happened in great detail. Vicky supplying other facts, and then she shared what Jerome had told her about the suspect. Out of respect for his confidence, she didn't say the name, but she felt it was important that the club know the extent of the viable suspect.

Even before she was finished sharing about Casey, she could tell most of the group thought it was too easy.

"There's always at least a few suspects to run through in books," Willard pointed out, licking powdered sugar from his fingers.

"This isn't exactly a novel," Pete said, with an eyeroll.

"No, but he has a point," Elijah interjected. "There *are* other suspects—I mean, anyone on that island is a suspect excluding Vicky and Eva so—"

"We're suspects too," Eva said, with a smile. "Let's rule us out."

Geraldine raised her hand with a finger pointed at them both. "No motive. No opportunity."

Everyone chuckled, but she was right.

"We do alibi each other out," Vicky pointed out. "But that's not to say we couldn't have done it together."

More laughter went around the circle but sobered quickly. It was one thing to laugh about the impossibility of someone you knew being a murderer, but there was a *real* murderer out there and that made everything much more serious.

"But you saw another man at the site of the body—in addition to the guy running away, right?" Kay asked.

"Yes," Eva said. She filled them in on his story, but even as she did something came back to her that felt wrong, and she hadn't realized it until then. "What I didn't catch during his interview was the fact that he said 'not really' when Jerome asked him if he'd seen the dead woman before."

Vicky turned to her. "Not really? That's not an answer."

"Exactly."

"He goes on the list," Pete said, pulling out a notebook.

Eva wanted to smile again, but she also didn't want to hinder Pete's enthusiasm. Whatever had happened between their last case and this one, she liked this side of Pete.

"And don't forget to add that woman and the big guy," Geraldine's nose scrunched. "Uh Tina and Lin?"

"Lilly and Tim," Eva said with a chuckle. She had described everyone as best she could, and despite not using the word 'hulk' in her description of Tim, Geraldine wasn't far off in the descriptor.

"Whoever they are, they don't seem to fit the mold of visitors to a nature preserve. At least not the man. I'd be looking at them if I was that handsome detective."

"Who else?" Elijah said, peering over at Pete's paper.

"If we're listing everyone, then we need to add the visitor's employees, the fish and wildlife officer, the woman and her son—she walked past us, right Vicky?" Eva said, getting an affirming nod from the woman. "And perhaps two other families. But I know one was already in the visitor center when we were all brought in, and the other family took the trail circling the island counterclockwise. I heard that they had to send out the guide to find them and bring them back. Due to the terrain of the island, I don't think it's logically possible they had anything to do with the murder."

"Got it," Pete said, making a few more notes.

"It's a small list, but still too big," Vicky said, biting her lip. "But, oh! How did I forget?"

"Forget what?" Elijah asked.

"I discovered something." She looked to Eva.

"You don't have to share if you think you shouldn't," she said, encouraging her friend to use her best judgment.

"I think it will turn out to be of little consequence, but it *is* something."

"Spit it out," Geraldine said.

"I found a note in the woman's hand."

"What did it say?" Willard asked.

"That's why I think it's not that big of a deal," Vicky admitted. "It was just a scrap, like someone had torn it away." Vicky grabbed a piece of paper from her purse and scribbled something. Then she held it up. The paper was blank except for one odd thing—:30. "There were a few other numbers, but they made no sense to me."

"Like, thirty, as in a time?"

"Exactly like that," Vicky said, nodding her head.

Eva leaned back. "Interesting."

"What? What is it?" Pete asked. "We know that look."

Eva tossed up her hands and laughed. "Apparently I

have all these looks. But I was just thinking that it seems more likely this woman was there for a specific purpose. If it was a pre-arranged meeting then…"

"The note could have been the time?"

"Yes," Eva said, nodding. "And perhaps the other numbers were the location of the meeting?"

Vicky stared back. "I hadn't thought of that."

"I'm sure Jerome will have an idea. Make sure he knows of this first thing tomorrow."

"Oh, don't you worry about that," Vicky assured her. "That's my job, after all."

"What I don't understand," Kay said, taking a sip from her coffee, "is who is this woman?"

Eva turned to her with a nod. "Which is, I think, the very first thing we need to uncover. Find out who the victim is, then we may know the motive for one of the suspects to want her dead."

"We're hoping to have an ID tomorrow," Vicky supplied.

"Good. Then we'll go from there," Eva said.

"Why don't you do what you did a few cases ago and assign us some people to look into?" Pete suggested.

"Good idea, honey," Kay said, squeezing his biceps.

"Okay, well…" Eva looked around the circle. "Why don't Vicky and I take the victim—she'll be busy so I'll do what I can. Then Elijah, why don't you look into Lilly and Tim—we'll get you their last names tomorrow. That leaves Willard looking into Darnell Forrester. Kay and Pete, since you'd mentioned ties to the wildlife refuge—you can look into the staff on the island, and Geraldine—

you look into the families. Mostly the woman and her son, though I have a feeling they'll turn up clean in all of this. I have a hard time believing a woman would take her son to an island just to murder someone."

They all agreed with her assignments, and then Eva turned to Vicky. "How about I come by in the morning and we chat?"

Vicky nodded. "We'll get to the bottom of this, I just know it."

7

MONDAY MORNING WAS as busy as usual and Eva was thankful that Jake had offered to step in to cover the morning checkouts as well as the new guests who were coming in, many of them for the week.

"The Hansen family has both the Green Room and the Teal Room. Don't forget to unlock the adjoining door before they arrive. I forgot to tell Elena." Eva rolled her eyes skyward trying to think of anything else she needed to share with Jake before she left.

"I've got it. Don't worry. I can call you if I need to though, right?"

"Call? Yes, of course." Eva drew her gaze back to the college student. "Sorry, Jake. I'm a little scattered this morning."

"No worries. I saw the news about the murder out at the Great White Heron preserve. You and Vicky were there, right?"

She blinked. "Were our names in the paper?"

"Um…" Jake grimaced. "You were mentioned."

Great. That was just what she needed, more publicity. "Thanks for letting me know."

"Don't worry—it was just a quick mention."

"At least this time there aren't a bunch of reporters out front," she said with a shake of her head.

"Good point. I'll see ya when you get back."

"Thanks again, Jake."

"No problem," he said with a big smile.

She headed out the front door, her woven tote and sun hat in hand. She paused on the porch to set her hat and make sure the car she'd arranged for was on its way. When it pulled up out front, she rushed down the steps and slipped into the cool interior. It wasn't nine o'clock yet and already the heat and humidity were rising. She fanned herself with the hat until the air-conditioning battled out the heat she'd let in by opening the door.

All too soon they were at the police station, and she climbed out, thanking the driver. She'd assumed that Vicky wouldn't want to see her until at least lunchtime, but she'd gotten a text from her friend that very morning to come over as soon as she could.

The interior of the police station was blessedly cool, and the temperature dropped as she reached the basement level where the morgue was located. Eva had been down here before, but it was never something she enjoyed.

Vicky had done what she could to spruce up the area with fake plants, an odd collection of movie posters—

most westerns—and even a Texas flag, but it didn't change the fact that it was very much a place for corpses and those who worked on them.

"You made it," Vicky said, smiling.

"Yes. It's early though. Surely you can't have anything yet."

Vicky looked slightly sheepish. "Well, I ended up coming back after the dinner at the B&B and stayed late to finish the autopsy."

"Are you serious?"

"I know." Vicky blushed. "My Mee-maw would call me a workaholic, but I had to know what happened to that poor lady."

"And?" Eva wasn't sure she wanted *all* the details, but she trusted her friend to give her the highlights at least.

"Strangulation with the strap, just like you'd thought."

Eva shook her head. It wasn't something she *wanted* to be right about, but it did help that they had the murder weapon.

"I assume it would take quite a bit of strength for that."

Vicky was silent for a few moments as she tilted her head to one side, then the other. She wore a bright orange dress with a large bow off to one side of her hip. Her black pumps had an edge of orange on them as well and Eva wondered if she only wore those shoes with this dress.

"Not exactly." Vicky made a face. "While it does take quite a bit of force, a strong woman could—in theory—do the same amount of damage. It would require a bit more leverage is all."

"Leverage enough to break the strap?"

"Possibly."

That didn't exactly narrow down the suspect pool, something Eva wasn't too happy about. Then again, if it were up to Jerome and his info yesterday, they might already have the man in custody.

"Did you tell Jerome this?"

"The report was on his desk this morning, but I haven't seen him yet. He's busier than a three-legged cattle dog."

Eva frowned, almost asking her what that even meant, when the door at the end of the hall opened. A handsome lab tech walked in, his blue coat denoting his station.

"Here are those reports you asked for Dr. Clem."

"Thank you, Shawn," Vicky said, blushing. She signed the papers and the man left. "What?" she said when she turned back to see Eva staring at her.

"*That's* Shawn?"

Vicky looked toward the door. "Yes. And?"

"He's…young." Eva couldn't keep the grin from forming. She knew Vicky was somewhere in her early forties and Shawn had to be in his early thirties if not late twenties.

"I told you it didn't work out." Vicky looked away, biting her lip.

Eva was about to rib her further when they both heard footsteps on the stairs. Soon, Jerome emerged from around the corner. He looked surprised to see Eva, but not as surprised as she might have guessed.

"I will assume that I interrupted something non-law enforcement related, right ladies?"

"Actually, we were just talking about ages in dating and—" Eva began.

"And nothing. Do you need something darlin'?" Vicky said, her Texan accent thickening the more flustered she felt.

"I wanted to discuss your findings but—" He turned to Eva. "Since you're here, that saves me a call."

"Oh?" She tried to look innocent.

"I'm sure our good ME here has given you the details of the method of death, but I wanted to let you know that what I called you about yesterday…" He rubbed at his neck. "Well, it was too good to be true."

"You mean your perfect suspect isn't the right one?" She tried so hard to keep the smile from her face, but it slipped at the end.

Jerome rolled his eyes. "Did you want to throw in an 'I told you so' or should I just assume it's been said?"

She merely smiled.

"So, you are back to the drawing board?" Vicky said, trying to get them back on track.

"Yeah." He looked less than pleased. "I mean, I wasn't putting much stock in it, honestly."

"Not what it sounded like on the phone," Eva said, keeping her tone even so as not to accuse him.

"Maybe I got a little carried away. It's not every day that you have a suspect handed to you. We haven't actually found him yet, but we're fairly certain he couldn't have committed the crime." Jerome turned to Vicky. "That's why I'm here."

"Oh?" She looked intrigued.

"Based on your report, I assume someone has to have two hands to do the, uh…" He sent Eva a quick glance.

"The strangling," she supplied. While she appreciated his candor and worry over a civilian getting too close to a murder, she wasn't so squeamish that she couldn't say a word. But observing a body was another matter. One she'd like to leave to Vicky and the police, thank you.

"Right. The strangling."

"As I was just telling—I mean…" Vicky cleared her throat. "I think the act could have been done by either a man or a strong woman, but leverage would be key. And yes, I believe two fully functioning hands would be necessary for this level of damage."

"That's what I thought." Jerome looked peeved.

"May I ask why that's important?" Vicky said.

"Because at the time of the murder, Casey Ferrington had a broken wrist and was in a cast. I had officers checking out his last known residence and that's where we learned he'd been in a fight. Talked to his doctor and got some X-rays that, according to them, would make it impossible for him to have the leverage you mention in the report."

"That would make it nearly impossible for him to be your suspect," Vicky agreed.

"Nearly impossible?" Eva asked.

"I won't say impossible until I examine the X-rays and

see the man and his cast, but I'm reasonably certain it wouldn't be possible."

"We'll work on getting that to you, Doc," Jerome said. "If you're heading out, I'll walk with you," he said to Eva.

She'd hoped to talk with Vicky about the victim and piece together who she was, but she also knew that Vicky would have other work she had to get to, and she didn't want Jerome to know about the sleuthing, at least not yet.

"Yes, that would be nice," she said, flashing Vicky a smile.

Vicky waved at her and slipped back into her office, and they took the stairs up to the front lobby area.

"Eva," Jerome began, right as she was heading toward the doors. "You're...not looking into this are you?"

It was the question she'd dreaded he'd ask, but the one she should have expected.

"What do you mean by—"

"You know what?" He held up a hand. "Never mind."

Her eyebrows rose and he shrugged in response. "Probably better not to know."

She turned back to the door and was almost there when he called out to her. "I've always fancied a woman a little younger than me."

"Pardon?" She turned to find him looking at her, amused.

"You said you and Vicky were talking about dating ages." He winked and disappeared through a door.

And despite her best efforts, she couldn't help the smile that took over at what he'd said.

THE MOMENT EVA walked in the front door of the Key's Bed and Breakfast, her phone dinged with an email. She'd stopped by one of her favorite coffee shops for an iced coffee and pastry and had spent time enjoying people watching rather than being on her phone. But now, work called.

She pulled her phone from her purse and swiped it open, navigating to her email app. Her stomach knotted when she saw the sender—it was the same person who'd emailed her several days before.

To: Eva Stewart <estewart@thekeysbandb.com>
From: <goodnitemoon536@xmail.com>
Subject: RE: Help!

MS. STEWART –

I'M afraid I never received a reply to my last email. I am in desperate need of your help. I know the cases you've helped solve in Key West and I know how smart you are. Please—please —*respond (just a yes will do) so I know you will help me.*

EVA MOVED her thumb to swipe the email into the trash but hesitated. She wasn't going to reply. After all, the email was worded so oddly, and she didn't get a good feeling about the whole situation, but that didn't mean that there was no alternative to a response.

"How'd it go?" Jake asked, passing her from the kitchen back to the front desk area. He settled into the plush leather office chair and set down a steaming cup of coffee.

"Good, but…" She looked at the message and back to Jake. "I have something else I need help with."

"Shoot." He took a careful sip and then gave her his full attention.

"I know you're taking classes and know quite a bit about computer technology." She stepped toward the desk, phone still held halfway in front of her. "But do you know much about email?"

His eyebrows rose. "Like…sending one or are we talking about something more than that."

She smiled. "I'm inept at most technological things, as you know, but I *can* manage to send and receive emails. I'm talking about a little more than that. Like tracing one back to its source."

"Oh." Jake sat up straighter. "I…I mean I could take a look at it. There are a few things I can do to trace the IP address."

"And that would be helpful?" She wasn't exactly sure what he was offering.

"Yes, I mean, in the sense that it would tell you where the sender is located and maybe a bit more information. It just depends on the encryption. Would that help?"

At this point, Eva was fairly certain anything more he could tell her would be more helpful than the odd emails.

"Yes, that would be great. I will say…" She looked down at the email. "The content is a little odd. I don't mind you seeing it, of course, but it's just a strange request from someone. They've contacted me twice now for my so-called sleuthing skills, though I don't know where they'd get the idea those are on offer." She chuckled.

"I got ya," Jake said, amicably. "Well, if I can see them both, I can look into them and let you know what I find out."

"That would be wonderful," she said. "Can I just log into my email on the office computer here?"

"That'd work."

She did, making sure to find the first archived email, and then headed off for her cottage. The midday lull was upon them, that odd time during and after lunch before it hit true afternoon but not too early to be a morning rush, and she felt like a small nap was in order. Something to help focus her thoughts.

Her phone dinged, though thankfully it was a text, not an email this time. When she checked it, she saw that it was Vicky and she wanted to come by in an hour to talk about the victim.

Eva sent off a quick reply agreeing to meet with her in the main area of the bed-and-breakfast and then went to her couch where a novel and a cool glass of water were just the things she needed to help focus her mind for this case.

AFTER A SHORT NAP, a snack, and a note from Jake saying that he'd need more time to look into the email, Eva entered the main room of the bed-and-breakfast a few minutes before Vicky was to show up.

"Hello Poirot," she said, approaching the large cage that housed her parrot.

"Pretty bird!" Poirot shuffled across one of his perches to come near one of the small windows she often used to feed him bird treats. "Pretty bird wants a treat!"

"You always want a treat," she said, smiling at the bird as he bobbed his head up and down in excitement.

Eva opened the small window and gave the bird an almond. They went through the routine of her requiring an action—shaking his leg, flapping his wings, or saying something—in exchange for a treat a few times until the front doorbell rang.

"I'm sorry I'm late," Vicky said, rushing in.

"It's all right, I was just doing treat-time with Poirot."

"Pretty bird!" he insisted from behind Eva.

"Let's go out onto the porch. I'll make sure the misters and fans are on."

"Sounds good to me," Vicky agreed, pouring herself a glass of water from the complimentary station before following Eva out to the porch.

"Sorry I left in a hurry this morning," Eva said when they were seated on the porch. The above fans sent the misted air swirling toward them in a delightful manner, making the heat bearable.

"Nonsense. I had work to do and best not to let Jerome

in on too much just yet." She smiled and then reached into her purse, pulling out a file.

"You didn't take that from work, did you?"

"It's all right," Vicky said, flashing a knowing smile back at Eva. "It's not a case file. Just a file folder. It's for anything we might hear about any of the suspects in this case. Plus, a few notes I took."

"What did you uncover?"

"Well…" Vicky opened the file. "The victims full name is Beth Marie Swanson. She was thirty-six, single, and not from the area. There was no immediate record of where she was staying, but she does have a sister in California that they are trying to get a hold of. And get this…" Vicky looked up, excitement coloring her cheeks. "She's a bird conservationist."

"Really?" Eva was shocked at the wealth of information her friend had gotten. Then again, being a medical examiner had its perks, if you could call it that.

"Yep. I thought that would be enough information to get us on track with Kay and Pete's contacts at the Wildlife Refuge. Perhaps they'll know where she was staying or Jerome will uncover it first."

Eva stood and paced to the porch railing and back. Her mind was whirring with possibilities. "She was visiting then, so it would seem?"

"Looks that way."

"Then the first question is—was it a crime of opportunity, like Jerome thought, though not with the culprit he'd assumed it might be. Or was it more planned than that. And if it was planned, then why at the refuge? It seems to link her work to her killer, doesn't it?"

"It could. Or perhaps it's unrelated to her work but personal life?"

"I think it would be odd that someone would bother to follow her all the way to the Keys just to murder her." Then again, was murder so rational? "It would seem there's a lot of research for us to do."

"Yes but…" Vicky checked her watch. "I've got to skedaddle to my afternoon yoga class."

"That's new," Eva said, standing to walk her friend to the door.

"It is. Shawn suggested it."

"I thought you weren't seeing him anymore."

"I didn't say that," Vicky said with a girlish laugh. "Just that our date wasn't…great. He's a nice guy. Honestly, I'm not sure if we're relationship material, but he's getting me a guest pass to this new studio, so I'll try it out and see what I think."

It was on the tip of Eva's tongue to say something about caution, but she held it in. Vicky was a grown woman, and able to make her own decisions regarding the men in her life.

"I'll see ya, darlin'," she said with a quick air kiss to Eva's cheek before she rushed out the door.

Eva watched her go with an amused smile.

Then her thoughts shifted to the victim—Beth—and how she'd been visiting Florida and would never return to her family again. It was devastating to think of, but the tragedy pushed Eva even more toward uncovering the woman's killer. There would be justice for Beth, and she wanted to make sure it happened as quickly as possible.

But first, she had to put in a call to Pete and Kay to see if their contacts could come up with anything regarding Beth.

8

THE OPEN-AIR CAFÉ bustled with activity and a beautiful view of the ocean. Eva sat with Kay and Pete, all enjoying coffee and treats. They had arranged a quick meeting to discuss what the couple had uncovered while talking to their connections at the refuge.

"Bill is the one I went to high school with. He said she was only supposed to be here for two weeks," Pete said, finishing his coffee.

"That's not much time."

"No, but it could be why they can't find where she was staying."

"I'm shocked they didn't find a purse on her," Kay interjected, taking a bite of her blueberry scone. "I mean, what woman is caught dead without her purse?" The moment she said it she squeaked and placed a hand over her mouth. "I—I didn't mean to say it like that."

"It's all right," Eva assured her. "It's a figure of speech."

"She's got a point though," Pete said. "The killer must have taken it."

"Good to know if they do find a viable suspect," Eva mused. It had only been a day since they uncovered the woman's identity, but according to Vicky, Jerome still had no idea where Beth had been staying and her sister, while coming in from California the next day, hadn't known of her travel plans either.

"It is odd though, isn't it?" Kay said.

"What, dear?" Pete replied.

"That they couldn't trace her credit card to where she was staying."

Eva had considered this strange as well. "It's almost as if she didn't want anyone to know where she was staying once she got to Florida. A plane ticket is difficult to buy without being traced."

"You think she was on the run from something?" Pete said, jumping to conclusions.

"No," Eva said, then amended, "well, perhaps not. There are many reasons someone may not want to have their whereabouts traced."

"But to have her end up...dead?" Kay suppressed a shiver. "It's horrible."

"It is," Eva agreed.

"Are you helping Elijah today?" Pete asked out of the blue.

"I was planning on it," Eva said, finishing her last sip of coffee. "Vicky's supposed to meet us here and then we're heading over when we're done.

"We wanted to help, but we double-booked ourselves,

so we have to both cut and wash or else we'd be there." Pete finished off his pastry. "I wonder if he's had any luck figuring much out about the woman and man?"

"I was wondering the same thing," Eva admitted. "He's got a lot of friends around the island, but it's hard to know where to start."

"Hard because we're not the police," Pete pointed out.

"True," Eva said.

She'd been thinking about calling Jerome, but it felt a little too obvious to check in so soon after she'd just seen him. Then again, he was becoming more and more accustomed to her sleuthing as well as involving the Murder Mystery Book Club and she had to wonder if he minded their theories, as long as they didn't interfere.

"There you are," Vicky said, making her way through the tables. A light breeze blew her sundress around her ankles, the large prints of sunflowers dancing around her. "Sorry I'm late, y'all." She slipped into a seat, reaching up to smooth out her blonde hair.

"We're almost done," Kay said, looking sheepish. "We have to get back to the business soon, so we didn't wait. Sorry about that."

"It's fine." Vicky waved a hand, her manicured nails flashing. "Don't apologize. We landed another case this morning, so I've been working double time. Not a murder, thankfully." She dropped her voice as if realizing where they were.

"I don't know how you do it," Kay said, looking a little green around the edges at the mere thought of Vicky's job.

"I hate to say you get used to it…but you kinda do." She shrugged and eyed the pastries in the glass cabinet through the open doors into the café. "I'll be right back."

"I wouldn't be able to eat for a week if I had her job," Kay said.

Pete laughed. "You *wouldn't* have her job—you're too passionate about animals."

Considering that Kay was wearing a navy-blue romper with pawprints all over it, Eva had to agree with her husband. Kay was passionate about her job which would lead her to do almost anything for it. She loved animals and their grooming, but she also cared about them being treated well.

And something in that line of thinking struck a chord with Eva. Being passionate about a job could lead a person to do all sorts of things. Was it possible that Beth had fallen into something connected to her job and it somehow resulted in her murder?

"Kay, Pete," Eva began, and they both turned to look at her. "In your research into the Great White Heron Wildlife Refuge, did you find out about anything odd going on? Perhaps any activist groups or scandals or anything surrounding the refuge that might be tied into Beth's murder?"

Pete shrugged. "Talking with Bill, he seemed to think that there was no earthly reason that someone would be killed on that refuge. I mean, it's about birds—what's controversial about that?"

"True," Eva said, nodding. "It was just a thought."

"I could reach out to Ethel," Kay said, straightening in

her chair. She looked excited and her eyes began to sparkle.

"Are you sure you're up for that, honey?" Pete said, looking less enthusiastic.

"Who is Ethel?" Eva asked.

"Pete and I used to be..." Kay shrugged. "Well, we would fight for animal rights."

"You were activists?" Eva said, feigning shock. She couldn't see them doing anything that would harm anyone else.

"In a sense. I was really passionate in college where I first met Ethel up in Miami, but I kind of distanced myself to get a job afterward. Then I met up with Pete at a rally and things kind of, you know, heated up again on that front. It turned out that Ethel was heading up one of our marches and we reconnected."

"She lives down here?" Eva asked.

"No, she travels around Florida and sometimes all over the U.S., but the last time we connected with her, things were getting close to out of hand, you know?"

Eva didn't, but she gestured for Kay to continue.

"We were just starting up our grooming business so we made a decision to do whatever we could to support efforts we believed in, but nothing that was too radical. We didn't want to alienate clients."

"I see. But you think this Ethel may know of something local?"

"I'll admit it's a stretch," Kay agreed, her head bobbing. "But I think if there was something happening at the refuge, she'd be the one to know about it or to find out about it."

"I don't want you to risk involvement in something you don't feel comfortable about," Eva said. She knew that there were certain things in her past she wanted distance from and would never push others in a way she wouldn't push herself.

"I think it would be all right." Kay looked to Pete. "We've actually been on our own for a while now and I'm proud of how we stand up for what we believe. I don't think we feel the need to be extreme, but I think Ethel will respect that."

"Then yes, call her."

"Call who?" Vicky said, setting down her to-go cup of coffee and pastry wrapped in a white paper bag.

"Long story," Eva said. "I'll tell you on the way to Elijah's gallery."

Vicky shrugged and dug out a piece of a chocolate chip cookie, not even bothering to sit down now that Eva was standing up.

"Thanks for meeting me here you guys," Eva said, standing as well and collecting her purse, hat, and camera bag.

"Of course," Pete said, still looking like he'd caught the mystery solving bug. "We'll, let you know anything we uncover."

"Perfect." Eva offered them a small wave and then turned to Vicky. "Ready to go?"

She grinned, chocolate on her lips. "Lead the way."

THE PIERSON GALLERY was adjacent to several others along a strip of shops boasting upscale artwork. It was a good location and the window space, currently empty, would afford Elijah a great feature area for his work. The Pierson worked on an installation-by-installation basis where an artist would 'take over' the entire gallery for a set amount of time.

This ensured not only was there no competition between artists, but it created a kind of 'winner take all' mentality that often sold paintings more quickly than other avenues.

"I'm impressed by this space," Eva said, turning around in a slow circle to take in the room. It was large and open, but the owner had set up moveable panels to allow for a flow to the room. The lighting would also be specially positioned to focus on the art pieces Elijah chose, and the natural light during the day would only make his pieces more inviting.

The space itself had a high-class feel to it and Eva immediately knew this gallery exhibit would be wonderful for her artist friend. She envisioned the photographs Elijah wanted her to take and felt her fingers itching for her camera. A feeling that had gone away after the tragedy at the wildlife refuge.

"Elijah, this is going to be amazing," Vicky said, spinning much in the same way Eva had. "Do you have enough to fill the space?"

"Actually, I have more than enough since they want

both types of my art. I did have an idea I wanted to run by you both though." He looked between them and, when they both gave him nods, he rushed on. "I was thinking, since the room is naturally divided in half, that I might split up my styles the same way. I don't want it to be jarring, of course, but I think it would make more sense to see a flow of my style rather than have everything at odds with one another."

Eva tilted her head to the side, trying to envision what he was saying.

"I was thinking I'd start here to the left of the door with my early modern work." He moved toward the back but still on the left side of the gallery. "Then here, I'd feature the transition pieces. The ones that more heavily lean toward impressionism but still hold a hint of modernism would go here." He moved across to the right half of the gallery. "And then my most recent impressionist works would be here at the front."

"I like it," Vicky said, bobbing her head. She wasn't really into art, as she'd made sure to tell Eva on their way over, but she was more than happy to come and support a friend.

"I think it's a brilliant idea," Eva said. She could easily envision what he was talking about. "It would bring your viewers on a unique journey."

"That's what I was hoping."

"What do you need us to do?" Vicky asked, tossing her coffee cup and bag in the trash.

"I rented a van and brought several of my paintings, all labeled. I sketched out a rough draft of where everything will go. We can unload and reference the sketch to see where to put them."

"Sounds good."

Elijah nodded, flashing Vicky a wide smile, and then motioned for them to follow him out the back door of the gallery where a white panel van was parked. When he opened the back, they could see a row of stacked boxes, all with labels on the side designating the title of the piece.

Elijah pulled out the first painting and handed it to Eva who took it inside to reference the map Elijah had drawn. Finding its location, she took it over and propped it up against the wall before going back to the van for the next painting.

With all three of them working, it didn't take long to unload the van.

"Thanks guys. I think Kay and Pete will be able to make it tomorrow to help with the rest."

"Do you need help hanging them?" Eva asked.

"No, the gallery actually has a guy who comes in to do that, but they wanted them set up first. We're about halfway there."

"I'm so excited for you," Vicky said, bounding up on the balls of her feet like a child.

Elijah laughed. "Thanks V. Hey, do you guys want some water?"

He handed out bottled waters from a small fridge in the break area of the gallery and they looked around the room.

"When is your opening?" Eva asked.

"Should be in about a week, I think? We're putting all

the details together now. We'll open around four in the afternoon and then host the big opening party later that night."

"I was hoping you'd say that," Eva said. "I think the lighting in here will be perfect in the late afternoon, so if I can come in an hour ahead of the opening for photos, that would be great. But then I'll stick around to take a few more pictures when the guests start showing up."

"Sounds perfect." Elijah took a swig of his water as Eva pulled out her camera and began working on settings for inside of the gallery.

"Did you find out anything about that couple from the island?" Vicky asked as Eva moved from one spot to the next, snapping pictures.

"Not yet," Elijah admitted. To Eva, he sounded a little sheepish. "I've been so busy with the installation…"

"Understandable," Eva said, pulling her camera away from her face. "You've got a lot on your plate. Maybe you can help us with one aspect though."

"What's that?" Elijah looked between Eva and Vicky.

"We found out who the woman is. Her name is Beth Swanson, and we can't seem to find where she was staying. I don't know that the police have found it yet either." Eva looked to Vicky who nodded in agreement with her statement. "We thought you might have some ideas. I remember when you first moved here you stayed at a lot of different places and—"

Elijah's laugh interrupted her. "Are you getting on me for couch surfing, Eva?"

"You couch surfed?" Vicky propped a hand on her hip,

her grin widening. "I thought you sold a lot of those modern pieces?" She was tactfully saying she knew Elijah had done well for himself during his time in San Francisco as a modern artist.

"I had, but I'm also an artist—a free spirit—and I wanted to make sure that Key West was where I wanted to settle down. It's a lot easier to do that when you're seeing the real part of the city, not just the fancy hotels or Airbnbs."

"Do you have any ideas then?" Eva explained.

Elijah thought for a moment, his eyes rolling to the ceiling in thought. "I mean there are probably a hundred places in Key West but…"

"She would have been paying in cash."

"Cash?" Elijah turned his gaze to Eva. "And I'm assuming not a fancy place?"

"She was a conservationist. We don't think she was into fancy."

"I have a few places in mind. Why don't I check in with them and get back to you?"

"Do you have time for that?" Eva was concerned he wouldn't be ready for his opening if he spent too much time on the case.

"Oh sure, it won't take too long and with everyone's help, things are shaping up nicely. I'll let you know."

"Just make sure you don't mention anything about the murder," Eva pointed out. "If we do happen to find where Beth lived, we'll make sure Jerome is involved."

"You got it." He walked them to the door. "Thanks again for the help, ladies. You'll be here for the opening?"

"You betcha," Vicky said with a wink.

"Definitely."

"I'll be in touch." Elijah waved them off and Vicky hailed a cab for them.

Once in the air-conditioned seats, she turned to Eva. "Do you think he'll be able to succeed where the police haven't?"

"Normally I'd say no, but Elijah has a lot of connections. He lived on the beach for at least a week during the time I mentioned and met all sorts of people. You'd think he was a local for the amount of people he knows."

"Then let's hope he finds what we need."

Eva nodded as her phone vibrated to life in her purse. Pulling it out, she checked the caller ID to see that it was Ruben.

"Hello?"

"Ah, *dulzura,* I finally reach you."

"Have you been trying to call?"

"Um…" He hesitated. "I did stop by yesterday. Did Jake not tell you this?"

"He didn't." She made a face and Vicky gestured as if asking what was wrong. "I'm sorry."

"It is no matter. I want to have coffee with you. Soon!"

"Well…" She checked her mental calendar. "I assume you've got jobs this week so, Saturday morning perhaps?"

"*Perfecto.* That will be wonderful."

"I will text you with the location. I found a new little shop I want to try."

"Sounds good. See you then."

"*Adios*."

Ruben hung up and Eva turned to see Vicky's expectant look. "What?"

"Making dates on Saturday, are we? Was that Jerome?"

Eva's eyebrows rose. "Jer—why would it be Detective Makos?"

"Ha!" Vicky laughed. "Don't stand on formality with me, darlin'. I've seen the way you two interact. I mean, he let you come to the scene of the crime. That doesn't happen with just anyone."

"Perhaps it was just him recognizing me as an interested party. Like a private detective, of sorts." She tried to keep her squirming to a minimum. She *wasn't* licensed anymore, but Vicky didn't need to know that she was at one point.

"Maybe," Vicky said, grinning still. "But I'd bet its more than that. On both sides."

"Do I need to bring up Shawn again?" Eva said, laughing at the flush in Vicky's cheeks. "By the way, how was *yoga*?"

"Not for me." Vicky held up a hand, shaking her head. "I thought I'd like it. It's all the rage, you know? But nope. I need a little more *punch* in my workouts."

"Punch?"

"Something more active than stretching. I'm sure it's great for some, just not for me."

The cab pulled up to the Key's Bed and Breakfast, and Eva paid the man for her share of the fare. "Well, either way, the coffee with Ruben is just that—coffee."

"Ruben. Oh, I see how it is."

"You don't see a thing," Eva said, laughing as she stepped from the cab. "I am busy enough with my business and a rambunctious book club that moonlights as crime solvers, thank you."

Vicky waved her off. "Oh fine. You're no fun. I'll see you later."

"Bye."

Eva watched the cab pull away before she turned back to the B&B. It was time to spend a few precious hours working, because she had a feeling things with this case were close to opening up soon.

9

EVA SNAPPED another picture of the storm clouds on the horizon as they made their way toward Key West. She'd woken up early and after taking care of some business, she'd decided a trip to the beach with her camera was in order. It was the perfect day for it too.

While it was still early and the beach was mostly uninhabited, the clouds were the real show that morning. The sun streaming through from behind them added just the right touch of light, and Eva was starting to be happy with the photos she was getting.

A dog raced by her followed by its owner, a younger man wearing running shorts and a tank top. He waved at her, headphones blaring music as he dashed past. She waited until he was down the beach far enough to be part of the view and she snapped a photo.

"Do I need to arrest you for spying?" a voice said behind her. She spun around to find Jerome there, wearing khaki shorts and a button up shirt, looking relaxed and at peace on the beach.

She laughed. "No, he just made for an interesting focal point down the beach is all. I don't think you could make out his features if you tried."

"All right," he said, holding up his hands. "I'll accept that as your defense."

"You'd better, *detective.*" She offered a smile and stuffed her camera in her bag. "What are you doing out here? Aren't you supposed to be working or something?" She kept her tone light and could see that Jerome caught her teasing.

"I was up late. Caught another case and decided to let myself go in a little later today. You?"

"Well, as busy as my bed and breakfast can be, we're actually fully booked at the moment, so no one is coming or going. I've got my housekeeper working most of the day today, so I'll just be on call."

"Must be nice being your own boss," he commented with a smile.

"You seem to do all right, too."

He shrugged. "I suppose. You know why I came to Key West, Eva?"

"I think you mentioned something about hoping to retire here. Guess you want a slower pace of life?"

He took in the clouds, rubbing his hand along his jaw covered in day-old stubble. "It's peaceful here—when there isn't a murder."

She turned to look at him and could see the lines of worry that edged his eyes and forehead. "Any luck on that?" She was tentative to ask, but she also made sure her tone was conversational. A question he could ignore or accept depending on how he felt.

"Actually, things are a little stymied on that front."

"How so?"

"We still can't seem to find where the victim was staying while she was here and we're striking out with suspects that were on the island. Obviously, you and Vicky were cleared." He winked at her and she feigned looking relieved. "But the likely culprit didn't work out, as I mentioned before, and the park staff seems not to have any real reasons for hurting a conservationist. It would appear they were on the same team."

"Naturally," Eva said. They fell into step together walking up the beach.

"But there is a connection we hadn't made before."

Eva held her breath. Would he share with her what that connection was?

"That man, Darnell—he actually knew the victim."

Eva hid her joy that he'd shared and responded saying, "He did?"

"Well, something wasn't right when I was interviewing him and—"

"Was it when he said 'not really' about seeing the woman before?"

Jerome looked at her with surprise. "You caught that too?"

"I did."

"Good catch," he said. "I looked into it, and it turns out

not only did Darnell *know* Beth—the victim—but they dated."

"Really? For how long?"

"About a year."

"Long distance, then?"

He looked over at her in surprise. "Has Vicky been talking?"

"I'm sure she hasn't shared anything more than what I could have found on my own with a little research."

It was true, Vicky had told them things about the victim, but with Facebook and Jake's prowess online, they could have uncovered most of what she'd shared.

"I suppose that's true." He looked at her for a moment longer before turning back to the water. "Anyway, I interviewed him yesterday and he admitted to the relationship. When I pressed him about why he hadn't said anything during our interview before he said he was afraid."

"Because he'd hurt her?"

"No, because she'd been found dead." Jerome made a noise which let her know what he thought about that. "Either way, we're digging into his background. It would appear that the breakup was less than civil."

"And close relationships are always the first thing to consider when dealing with murder."

"True."

They walked on in silence for a few minutes, pausing for Eva to snap a shot of more cloud cover, before they reached the path that would lead to the street.

"I'm assuming the mother and son were cleared?" she said as they approached the street with traffic picking up.

Jerome laughed. "Actually, funny you should mention it. I brought them in for questioning. The father came with them, and I guess the woman didn't tell him what was going on and he confessed to losing his job right there in the interrogation room. The wife blew up and the kid looked stunned. It was...quite the moment."

"That's terrible," Eva said, gripping the handle of her camera bag.

"It ended well though, especially when the father realized it was about a murder and he'd made it about himself. I think she forgave him. That was my suggestion, at least. That, and I suggested the man buy his wife a dozen roses and get on that search for a new job."

Eva smiled. "You're a bit of a romantic, aren't you?"

"I suppose," Jerome said, with a shrug. "I just think the romance in a relationship should never end."

When he turned to look down at her, there was something behind his eyes that made the breath in Eva's lungs catch. An intensity she hadn't expected.

Then again, Jerome was an intense person in general. She was certain he couldn't help but be that way due to his job.

"It was nice running into you, Jerome," she said, when a cab pulled over.

"You too. I'm glad to see you're still taking photos." He nodded toward her camera.

"Perhaps it's sad that I have to say this but..." She

shrugged. "One dead body won't stop me from photography."

"I'm glad to hear it," Jerome said.

She closed the door to his laugher and settled back in her seat. It *had* been nice running into him and enjoying the easy way with which their conversation flowed. They could be talking about murder, photography, or a host of other things and it wouldn't matter. He would still be engaged on all fronts.

And she appreciated the fact that he seemed to trust her with case information. She wasn't sure how long it would last—especially if she brought something to his attention that came from the MMBC's investigation—but she'd cross that bridge when—or if—they got to it.

THE REST of the week flew by until Friday hit and the excitement of seeing the book club members peaked. Eva found herself rushing through the check-out process with guests, wishing them well, but tapping her foot in subtle impatience as they left and new guests came in for the weekend.

Benita needed to take a half day that day, and while she was like the lifeblood of the bed-and-breakfast, Eva knew it was more important for her to feel comfortable getting time off when she needed it. Eva would do everything she could to keep the housekeeper happy. She not only managed the front desk most days, but helped Anton plan breakfasts, helped Elena with rooms when the need was pressing, and kept everything looking good inside.

Outside, Paz was always busy with his gardening projects or with taking care of Poirot, but other than that, it was Benita. Eva was planning on giving the girl a raise the next month and couldn't wait to tell her.

"Eva?" a young woman said, her smile faltering.

"I'm sorry," Eva said, shaking off her distraction. "I think I was in another world. How can I help you Mrs. Collins?"

"I was just wondering if we could get an extra towel. Mike likes to have two." She rolled her eyes. "As if he has enough hair for that."

The women shared a smile and Eva walked over to the housekeeping closet to retrieve an extra towel. "Not a problem. He can have as many towels as he'd like."

"Thank you. We're so happy to be back here for our one-year anniversary."

"It's hard to believe it's already been a year," Eva said, remembering the couple had come to the B&B on their honeymoon travels.

"I know. But we plan to make it a tradition to come here. We just love this place."

"And we love having you."

She sent the woman off with her extra towel and took a seat behind her computer. She noticed that Jake was still signed into her private email on a tab, and she considered closing it, but before she did, she shot a text to the boy. He wasn't working that day, but he always seemed to have his phone with him.

. . .

EVA: Jake, do you still need my email open on the office computer?

JAKE: Sorry, Eva! I forgot to tell you I left it open. If you don't mind, can you keep it up? I ran into some weird stuff.

Eva: Weird? How so?

Jake: Encryption I haven't seen before. I blacked out the text, but I brought a printout of the source to one of my teachers—hope you don't mind.

Eva: No problem. Can they help?

Jake: Meeting with him in twenty minutes. I'll let you know.

Eva: Thanks, Jake!

Jake: No prob!

EVA SET her phone down and tapped open another screen. It was odd that Jake would have such trouble with the email. In the first one she'd gotten, the sender had seemed sure the email could be hacked. But Jake was saying it was encrypted. What was that all about?

Pushing thoughts of the strange email aside, Eva thought over the case they'd discuss that night. They had agreed to push their discussion of the book until the end of the meeting seeing as there was case information to be shared, but Eva felt impatient.

With a look at their possible suspects list, she could already cross off several. Casey was a no-go, the park employees seemed to be cleared, the woman and her son were off the list, as were she and Vicky. It left Darnell, who'd had a relationship with the victim that ended badly and was something he *hadn't* brought up to the police, and then there was Lily and Tim.

Eva was close to messaging Elijah to see if he'd had any luck on where Beth might have been staying but held back. He would either let them know before the meeting or at if he'd had any luck. Then they'd need to get Jerome involved. Seeing as how he had willingly let her know about where the case was at so far, she wondered if bringing him the woman's housing arrangement could open even more doors for communication between the club and the police station?

Then again, she had no idea if they'd be interested in that. Sure, they could use consultants for crime solving, but she'd never heard of a police department or a detective working with a murder mystery book club. Eva stifled a laugh at the very thought.

The door opened, and Anton came in carrying two shopping bags.

"Hello Eva," he said, closing the door gently with a well-placed shove of a foot.

"Anton, what are you doing shopping for food?" It was something she'd sourced out to a local boy who was always looking for odd jobs. Anton created the list and she paid a boy, Henry, to do the shopping for them.

"Henry was sick this week, and I wanted to do something special for brunch tomorrow."

"Oh." Eva shook her head "I almost forgot about Saturday brunch."

It was a new thing that Anton had suggested. Doing a regular, but light, breakfast for any guests who wanted it, but then offering a larger Saturday brunch as an option for those who wanted to sleep in.

It was in the testing phase, but due to the space available, he had even petitioned Eva to consider opening it up to other patrons, not just guests of the bed-and-breakfast. She wanted to see Anton's culinary skills shown off to as many people as possible. The idea of bringing in outside guests for brunch was appealing, but there were things to consider like table space, reservations, and opening up the B&B to outsiders while guests were staying there.

Due to the concerns, Eva and Anton had agreed to start with brunch for the guests and see how that went. This would be their first official week for it.

"Poor Henry," she said, standing. "Do you need help?"

"Nah." Anton shook his head, dark hair falling in front of his eyes for a moment before he shook it away. "But I did want to ask if you included the fliers in the guest's packets?"

"Yep! We already have several people interested."

"Good." His grin widened.

"Do you really think it's going to work?" She was trying to gauge Anton's interest.

"Ms. S, I've been in the Key's since I was a kid. You

know I know more people here than everyone *you've* met!" He winked at her. "If Anton starts a brunch, you can bet people will come."

She felt reassured by his confidence but couldn't help but laugh that he talked about himself in the third person.

"So, I have nothing to do with it?" she quipped.

"A little." He held his grin for a good five seconds before it burst forward, white teeth against tanned skin.

"All right. If Anton says so…" she trailed off.

"He does."

"Then I wish you the best."

"Thank you, Ms. S."

She smiled at the name he always called her and watched him carry all of his food supplies toward the kitchen. She wasn't one to be hesitant when it came to matters of business. She usually evaluated the risk, did the math, and then either went ahead with it or didn't, depending on the evaluation.

This was a little different. She had to trust that Anton's sway in Key West would get them the business he said it would but also not interfere too much with her bed-and-breakfast. And of course, this venture could not bother her guests.

She turned back to the computer and bought up a search engine. She was going to search for other hotels and restaurants that offered a Saturday brunch, considering that hosting it on Sunday would be more profitable, but then her mind did a type of misstep.

While she hadn't heard from Kay and Pete about their contacts that might link the woman to the conservation opportunities in the area, she hadn't really looked into it. Perhaps it was the fact that she was thinking ahead to their meeting in a few hours, or maybe she was bored, or perhaps a combination of each, but Eva clicked in the search bar and typed in the Great White Heron National Wildlife Refuge and conservation opportunities.

The search took her to a page that listed current and upcoming opportunities, of which there were only six, three current and three upcoming.

The first showed an end date at least three weeks prior and then the second was current with the third staring the next week. So, there was only one current opportunity. Clicking on the link, a new page opened, and she stared back at the woman from the visitor center—Lilly Quinn.

Eva blinked and began to read through the short article. Apparently, Lilly Quinn was a newt conservationist working on the refuge because in addition to being a good space for Great White Herons, it was also the perfect habitat for various species of newt.

According to the article, Lilly had come from a recent research trip to South America, and they were lucky to have her on the premises studying the various types of newts found there. Below her short biography, Eva found links to the species Lilly had already located and those she hoped to find.

Eva read the short stories about each type of newt and followed the links to more extensive pages about the creatures, many on Lilly's own website—newtsforlife.com. Before she knew it, Eva was on a rabbit trail of various types of newts, the conservation of them, and what would happen should specific types be found on the island.

As she hopped from one website to another, one article stuck out to her. It talked about a handful of rare newts and how some were running the risk of extension due to internet purchasing and smuggling. In most cases, these breeds were protected by special laws, but that didn't stop the smuggling, only hindered it a little.

Suddenly, the front door opened to the bed-and-breakfast and Eva jerked back from her computer like she'd been shocked. Laughing, she turned to find Elijah there, his usual rucksack slung over his shoulder and an easy-going grin on his handsome features.

"You startled me," she said, closing the internet browser but not ignoring what she'd found.

It was possible that Lilly's appearance with a South American goon-looking man at the scene of a crime wasn't an accident. Still, she realized her mind was running dangerously close to jumping to conclusions and she didn't want to do that.

"Sorry." Elijah pulled off his bag. "I'm a little early, but I couldn't look at my own artwork anymore," he laughed.

"How's the installation going?" she asked, coming out from behind the desk.

"I think I need a break from it. We open next week, but I need to clear my head, you know?"

She nodded. "I can understand that. I often need to step away from a project in order to come back to it with a fresh perspective."

"Exactly. Can I help you get ready for the meeting tonight?"

She smiled. "That would be great."

As she led him to the kitchen, making sure to stay out of Anton's way, they gathered all the supplies for drinks and the snacks she'd gathered together earlier, and made their way out onto the porch where misters and fans were already going at full force.

After placing everything in the right spots, he flopped onto a love seat and closed his eyes. "I'll be here until we start," he said, the hint of a smile on his lips.

She chose a couch opposite him and did the same, resisting the urge to ask him if he'd had any luck coming across where Beth may have rented a place. They had time to get to all that tonight.

For now, it was time to let her mind simmer over the things she'd learned from her online search and what she'd heard from Jerome and Vicky. If all went well, depending on what everyone else had to share, they might be that much closer to knowing more about Beth and her murder.

10

"IT IS JUST GHASTLY HOT," Geraldine said, making her entrance to the porch in the most dramatic fashion. She wore a long, loose fitting dress with a wide brimmed straw hat which she immediately pulled off. Her sunglasses were next. She sighed as she tossed them both onto the large wicker chair she planned to sit in. It was clear she was going to the drink station first.

"No hotter than usual," Willard said, fanning himself with a book from the coffee table. With his other hand, he picked up another deviled egg.

Elijah still occupied the chair he'd flopped on, though he'd shifted so Vicky could share the other half. Now they were just missing Kay and Pete.

Eva watched her friends as they interacted, Willard with the snacks, Geraldine with anyone who would converse with her about the weather, and Elijah and Vicky chatting occasionally, though Elijah didn't even open his eyes to answer.

Vicky looked nearly as tired as he did, and she wondered if it was another case that preoccupied her or if it was possible she knew more about Beth's case and wasn't going to be able to share. She often got that weighted look when there was something on her mind, but she couldn't talk about it.

"Hey all," Kay said, coming in with a fluff ball trailing her. Pete came in next, a similar fluff following him.

"Who do we have here?" Eva asked, looking at the dogs.

"Mario and Luigi," Pete said.

Everyone laughed.

"They are the sweetest boys," Kay said, ruffling the hair on both of their heads before sitting in the other love seat. Pete brought over two tall glasses of iced tea and took the seat next to her.

"Sorry we're late," Pete said. "Mario—"

"It was Luigi," Kay interrupted.

"One of the dogs stepped in gum and we had to do a little quick clipping." He rolled his eyes. "Got it out, but I'm afraid their owner won't be happy with the one sheered paw.

As Eva looked at the dogs, she could tell that one had a slight lack of hair on one paw. "It's barely noticeable," Eva said.

"You'd think that," Pete said, shaking his head, "but Mrs. Roberts is *quite* insistent on the particular grooming of her pets." He sounded like he was reciting something.

"Trim 'em all to look like that," Willard said, waving a

hand at the dogs. "It'll grow out evenly and she'll think it was supposed to be that way."

"That's not a bad idea," Kay said, nudging Pete in the arm.

"Thanks, Wil," Pete said with a grin toward the older man. Then he turned to Eva. "Time to discuss the case?"

Eva smiled, still surprised at whatever had gotten into Pete. He'd once been their most reluctant participant in case discussion, but now he seemed to be the most interested.

"Hear here," Geraldine said, shifting in her chair to tuck a leg up under her. "I'll go first."

Everyone turned toward her, and Eva grinned at her enthusiasm.

"Nothing. I learned absolutely nothing!" Everyone burst into laughter, and she waited until it died down. "All right, maybe not *nothing*."

"You had the families, right?" Eva said.

"Yes, and it was harder than you'd expect to get the information out of the taxi service to the island."

"Smart idea though," Vicky said.

"Yes, perhaps, but…" She tossed a hand to the side. "I had to take matters into my own hands."

"What does that mean?" Willard said, sipping from his Diet Coke.

"Sent the boy on an errand to find something I lost." She winked dramatically. "Once he was gone, I looked at his notes on the computer."

"Geraldine!" Kay said, shocked.

"It's not like I'm using the information for nefarious

purposes. It turns out there were only three families, like you said, Eva, and two of them were from out of town. I didn't expect them to be the ones who'd done something, but I do prefer to be thorough."

"Aren't we so lucky," Willard murmured. It was clear Geraldine heard him but chose to ignore him.

"The one family that was local was the woman and her son."

"And they weren't involved," Eva said.

Now everyone turned to look at her, and she shrugged. "I ran into Jerome on the beach, and he let it slip. He'd brought them in for questioning and the husband was merely hiding the fact he hadn't told his wife he'd lost his job. Dead end."

Everyone but Vicky seemed to accept the fact that she'd run into Jerome on the beach, but Vicky's eyes bored into her as if to say, *We'll discuss this later.*

"Who's next?" Geraldine asked.

"Not much to say about Darnell. I couldn't find much about him online except that he's a professor at some online college working in conservation." Willard shrugged.

"That, and he dated Beth, the victim," Eva said. Again, all eyes shot to her. "I'm sorry, perhaps I should have gone first."

"Let me guess, Jerome told you." Vicky barely managed to keep her smile from blossoming.

"As I said, I ran into him, and he happened to mention the story about the family and then about Darnell. All he said was that they were seeing each other."

"Anything else we need to know?" Geraldine asked. She didn't look unhappy, just curious.

"That was the gist of it."

"What about you, Elijah?" Vicky asked.

He reluctantly opened his eyes one at a time and then pushed himself to seating. "Sorry, I'm out of it tonight."

"Too much art?" Willard asked.

Elijah cracked a smile. "Something like that. But I do have some news."

Eva leaned forward. "Did you find where Beth was staying?"

"I think so." He held up his hands. "I'm not going to say definitively, but I asked around to my contacts and they said a woman recently rented a room from my friend, Yuki. She said the woman hadn't been back to her room since Sunday—which matches Beth—and that she was just waiting a few more days before going in and clearing any stuff out."

"Oh, she can't do that," Eva said.

"I know." Elijah held up a hand. "I'm just saying that's what she said. I told her to wait and that we'd stop by tomorrow to take a look."

"Oh, that's wonderful," Eva said.

Vicky held up a finger. "You mean…" She pointed to Elijah. "So you can tell Detective Makos."

"I figured we could take a quick look and—"

"No way." Vicky sounded adamant. "You need to bring the detective in on this."

"Do you know something we don't?" Pete asked, looking between Vicky and Eva.

"Not exactly," she said, twisting her napkin between her fingers. "I just think this is a bit more serious than we realize—than *I* do."

"What makes you say that?" Eva asked.

"It's all the chatter going around the department. Nothing specific, just that Beth's death seems to be linked to something bigger, but I don't know what."

"Newts?" Eva tried.

Vicky frowned. "What?"

"Well, this has nothing to do with Jerome, but I was doing some research before our meeting tonight and the couple I told you about—Lilly and Tim. It seems like Lilly is a newt expert."

"A what?" Willard looked between her and the rest of the group like someone was going to have to fill him in.

"Newts, you know, like geckos or...newts." Pete made motions with his hands, but Eva couldn't figure out what he was doing.

"Huh," Willard said, noncommittally.

"Anyway," Eva pressed on. "Lilly has pictures on the refuge's website and talks about her work in conservation of newts. Apparently, there are some newts that share the same environment as the Great White Heron. I did some deeper research and found that some newts are very valuable and can be smuggled."

"You think that someone killed off this lady because she caught them stealing newts?" Willard looked back at Eva.

"Not exactly, but I think there's a connection somewhere. I had this feeling about Lilly and her so-called friend. He looked South American, and they didn't act like they were dating. He seemed to be…protecting her."

"Maybe he was," Kay offered. "I mean, maybe her work is dangerous and he's protecting her."

Eva shrugged. "Maybe."

"So, who do we have left?" Geraldine said, pushing the conversation away from the newt option.

"The staff," Pete said. He shifted forward, the fluff at his feet—Eva thought it was Luigi—shifted position before resting its head down again. "We kind of hit a dead end there."

"How so?" Eva asked.

"Everyone seems to check out. I mean, we looked at all the employees on the island—there are only six and just three of them were present on the day of the murder. Granted, we don't have access to things like bank accounts, but Kay talked to one lady who seemed really shaken up about the whole thing. I managed to get on the phone with the other two by pretending to be a reporter, and they had nothing to add." Pete looked proud of himself.

"What about your contact? Ethel?" Eva asked.

"She still hasn't gotten back to us," Kay said. "She's a busy woman, but I hope to hear from her soon."

Eva nodded, her gaze moving to the billowing white curtains that separated their part of the deck from the rest of the porch. There wasn't much new information aside from Beth's possible living situation.

"Vicky's right," Eva finally said, returning to the

conversation. "We'll tell Jerome and see if he'll let a couple of us go with him to her possible living situation. Perhaps me and Elijah?"

Everyone nodded.

"And I'll text whatever we learn from Ethel," Kay added.

"But what about Lilly and Tim?" Geraldine said. "Shouldn't we look further into what they're about?"

"It doesn't seem like they'd have a reason to kill Beth," Vicky commented. "Beth was a bird conservationist, and they're focused on newts."

"But they overlap by both being on the island at the same time—perhaps even knew one another from their work there," Elijah pointed out.

"How about I keep digging?" Eva said. "If something comes up, we can look more personally into who they are. Maybe I'll get Jake in on it." She smiled to herself.

"Get him to come to our meetings too," Willard said.

Willard always wanted to expand their club to more members, but Eva didn't want Jake to feel pressure. She wasn't going to put anything on him aside from maybe a little searching—which she'd pay him for his time to do.

"Sounds like we have good forward motion. I know we're not exactly getting breakthroughs here, but hopefully by early next week we'll have more information."

Everyone nodded their agreement and Eva pulled out their latest book, The Hound of the Baskervilles by Arthur Conan Doyle. It was a bit of a departure from what they tended to read, but she found the change of pace in reading had been cathartic.

"Shall we start the club meeting then?"

Everyone nodded and picked up their book.

"The game's afoot," Willard said, then he went right back to munching on his chocolate chip cookie. Everyone laughed and settled into the conversation.

Eva let herself be transported to the West Country of England and the haunting, albeit supernatural, legend of the book's foundation. It was one thing to talk about real-life murder and another to posit Sherlock's techniques and all that Watson had to put up with.

But in the back of her mind, Eva wondered what Jerome would think of the progress they'd made with finding Beth's possible living situation. Hopefully, he'd overlook their presence in his case and instead take the assist like Watson would.

She smiled at that because Jerome was anything but a Watson character.

11

"I'M PRETENDING you aren't here," Jerome whispered to Elijah and Eva who stood behind him at the door to a small apartment at the back of Yuki Matsumoto's house. Apparently, it was a place she frequently rented out to artists or those in need of cheap, indiscriminate housing. She didn't ask questions as long as the rent was paid—in cash—every month.

"She said she was working at the Great White Heron Wildlife Refuge," Yuki said, stepping up behind them and unlocking the door. "I had no reason to doubt that."

"She was," Eva offered, but Jerome shot her a look as if to say—no need to give out more details.

"Thank you, Miss Matsumoto, we'll take it from here."

She shrugged, sending a *what can you do* look to Elijah, and then walked back down the palm-shaded path toward the main house muttering something to herself about police.

When she was gone, Jerome looked at them again.

"Don't touch anything. I need to see if this is the scene of a crime or just somewhere we'll gain more information about Miss Swanson.

They nodded, standing back, and watched as Jerome carefully opened the door, calling out *"Police"* even though everyone was positive no one was there. After waiting a few moments, he swung the door open, and they stepped into the space. It was small, only big enough for a bed, small seating area, kitchenette, and bathroom, but it was decorated in vibrant colors with a gallery wall of art above the bed.

"Nice place," Jerome muttered as he moved toward a black suitcase partially opened at the end of the bed.

"How do you expect to link her to this place?" Elijah asked. "Do you think she left her ID here when she went to the island?"

"Possibly," Jerome said, not looking up from where he was rooting through the suitcase. "There could be things here that would link back to her. You can look around but remember—don't touch."

He made eye contact with her, but she knew it wasn't because he thought she'd touch anything. She had a feeling he was hoping they'd help with the search to connect the woman to the apartment. And help they would.

She instructed Elijah to take the kitchen and she stepped into the small bathroom with a pedestal sink, tub, and toilet. There was a small bag of toiletries on a shelf above the toilet, and she peered in without touching. Toothbrush, toothpaste, and a small assortment of makeup. It was more like someone who might wear light eyeshadow and mascara, not a woman planning on putting on a full face of makeup. That fit with what she'd seen of Beth—though it was far from definitive.

Using a Kleenex, she opened the medicine cabinet and noticed a notepad and pen. She was about to close the door when something on the pen caught her attention. It was a small creature, looked like a newt, but next to it she saw a website address—newtsforlife.com.

Either Beth had known Lilly or they had met at one point, long enough for Beth to have one of the woman's promotional pens.

Then she caught sight of a hoodie through the mirror of the vanity. It was hanging up on the back of the door. It was the kind with a zip up front and there was a logo emblazoned on it. But she couldn't quite make out what it said. Was it possible it was also newt merchandise?

"Jerome?" she called out.

He stepped away from the suitcase and came to the bathroom. "See something?"

"I can't make out the logo and didn't want to disturb anything."

"Here." He'd pulled on gloves and moved the sweatshirt away so they could both read the full logo. It said Los Angeles National Wildlife Preserve. So nothing having to do with the newts.

"That's where she worked last," Jerome said, dropping the jacket back in place. "It's thin, but that may be enough to establish this as her home."

Eva was about to mention the pen to Jerome when

Elijah called from the main room.

"Guys?"

They came back out and he used his foot to point to something under the bed. It was the corner of a laptop. Jerome knelt down, and with a gloved hand, pulled it out. He lifted up the top and the screen went from black to showing an image of a bird in flight.

"Is it password protected?" Elijah asked.

Jerome tapped a key and then nodded. "Looks like it. We'll have to get someone from the tech department to—"

"Try Great White Heron with no spaces," Eva said on a whim.

He typed it in all lowercase and the screen came to life. "Nicely done, Ms. Stewart," Jerome said with a grin.

"I just took inspiration from her photo."

"I should have thought of that," he muttered, and Eva smiled.

Jerome took the laptop over to the table and tapped a few more keys. Eva and Elijah looked around the rest of the small apartment but couldn't find anything else of importance.

"Well, this is definitely Beth Swanson's computer," Jerome said, looking up from the screen. "It's registered to her. There's too much to go through here, but we'll look into it back at the station. Thanks for coming."

"You mean *not* coming," Elijah said with a grin.

"Sure." Jerome rolled his eyes and they followed him out of the room while he made a call to get technicians to the apartment. They needed to clean up the rest of her things and check for anything of importance.

"What happens next?" Elijah said when they were back at the front of Yuki's house.

"Next? You two leave so that when my team comes there are no questions as to what you're doing here." He flashed a bright smile and picked up his pen to make another note. The sight of it triggered Eva's memory. She was about to tell him about the pen in the bathroom when their car pulled up.

"Jerome—" she began, but his phone rang the next second.

By that time, Elijah was ushering her toward their car. Jerome waved and turned away as Elijah held the car door open.

"Did you need to catch him?" he asked before sliding in.

It was either a flimsy clue or it meant something, but Eva consoled herself with the fact that he was about to have a whole team there to tear apart the room. They'd find the pen and he could connect it with Lilly. She reminded herself that she didn't need to do his job for him.

"No," she said, moving over so Elijah had room. "Let's go."

The taxi pulled away from the curb and Eva checked her phone. She'd gotten a text, so she swiped open her phone and saw that it was from Ruben. For a moment, she was positive she'd forgotten their coffee date, but then she'd remembered. She'd rescheduled so she could give Anton her full attention at the brunch that had turned out both delicious and a big hit with her guests.

His text was short but confirmed that they were indeed meeting on Tuesday. She almost rolled her eyes but stopped herself because he had a point. She'd been hard to nail down on a date and it had nothing to do with the coffee so much as her thoughts were focused on this case. It seemed to grip her and not want to let her go.

Either way, she replied in the affirmative to his text and set another reminder—just in case.

"Sorry to stop by so early," Eva said.

"It's seven-thirty—that's not early," Geraldine said from where she stood next to a cage holding a little fur ball with bright eyes.

"She's right," Kay said. Her bright blue scrubs had little dogs and cats all over it, and she wore white clogs as she moved around the grooming tables in the interior of their shop. "We're up early in this place. They demand it." She grinned and put her arms out to showcase all of the animals. Most of the cages were full of small dogs and a few pens for cats as well.

While Pete and Kay focused on their dog grooming services, they also boarded animals of all kinds since they were passionate animal lovers.

"Where's Pete?" Geraldine said, sticking her finger in the cage so the dog could rub up against it.

"Aw, he likes you," Kay said.

"Pete?" Geraldine replied.

"No, Buttercup," she said, indicating the small dog.

"Please don't tell me someone named their dog—their *male* dog—Buttercup?" Geraldine said.

"They sure did," Pete said, coming in from a side door. He wore blue scrubs in a slightly darker color than Kay but without the animal additions. "What are you ladies doing here this morning?"

"I got Kay's text last night," Eva said. "Geraldine and I were supposed to have coffee, so we decided to make a visit."

"Glad to see you here," Pete said, scooping dog food into bowls on the back counter. "Want to tell her what we learned, Kay?"

"Not much, I'm afraid," Kay said, setting down the combs and brushes she was cleaning. "I had hoped that Elaine would have more to offer, but she mostly said that, while she'd communicated with Beth over email, she'd never met her."

"That's something," Eva said.

"True. She said that Beth was super passionate. She came all the way to Florida to work at the refuge, but on the side, she was investigating rumors of smuggling. Elaine thought she was interested in writing a book or maybe just a set of articles. She didn't know."

"Smuggling? Smuggling what?" Geraldine asked.

"Elaine wasn't sure. Apparently, there are a lot of valuable things in the Keys that people are willing to pay for."

"Such as?" Eva thought of the website about newts, but if there were multiple things, it could invalidate the tenuous connection with Lilly.

"Like tropical birds."

"Birds?" Geraldine said.

"Yes. She said there are certain types of parrots and other types of birds that are valuable in this area. People pay a lot of money for them, but it's also creating demand where the supply isn't able to keep up."

"You can just buy birds anywhere though," Geraldine said. "Isn't that how you got Poirot?"

"Yes, but I've heard about the value of certain birds. Was Elaine sure that's why Beth had come to Florida?"

"She seemed to be," Kay said, "but she didn't know much more than that."

"Thanks for this information." Eva took in a deep breath.

"What are you thinking?" Pete asked. He had finished feeding the indoor pets and came to stand next to Kay.

She filled them all in on the pen she'd found in Beth's bathroom and how she'd found a corresponding website. "It's not too much of a stretch to think that a woman like Beth—so passionate about protecting wildlife—might also connect with another preservationist like Lilly."

"Do you think Lilly actually knew her and didn't tell the police?" he asked.

"I think it's worth talking to Lilly about."

"Do you know where she is?" Kay asked.

"No." The room fell silent at Eva's admission.

"Vicky to the rescue! I'm sure she could get you an address," Geraldine pointed out.

Eva had considered this, but Vicky had acted strangely the last time she'd seen her, more cautious and wanting to involve Jerome at every turn. The last thing Eva wanted was to get her friend in trouble. But was there another way?

Even as she said it, the realization went off like a match in the dark. "I know how we can find out."

"How?" Kay and Pete said at the same time, smiling at each other after.

"The way I found her the first time. I'll get in touch with the wildlife refuge and see if they can put me in touch with her. After all, I've considered trying my hand at conservation work in the past…sort of." Geraldine let out a raspy laugh. "And if worse comes to worse, I'll donate to the cause. I *do* have a history of that."

She laughed at herself thinking of the money she'd donated during the course of a previous investigation. Then again, she *did* believe in preserving the wildlife in the Keys and found that the donation was something she was more than happy to do.

"Just be careful," Kay said. "I mean, if you meet with this lady and she *did* have something to do with Beth's murder…"

"I don't know if I think that." Eva wasn't really concerned about Lilly. It was more the man who was with her. "But I will be careful."

"I'll go with her," Geraldine offered.

Pete tried to hide a smile. "I'm sure that'll help," he muttered.

Geraldine shot him a look that would weaken nearly any man. "I may not be physically threatening, but I have a very sharp mind."

"And a sharp wit," Pete added.

It was Eva's turn to hide her smile. "Then let's get going. We'll get coffee, and I'll make the call."

"Good luck to you both," Kay said. "Let us know what happens."

"We will," Eva said as she held the door for Geraldine.

They walked back out into the warmth of the Florida morning. It wasn't even eight yet and already the humidity and heat were reading an uncomfortable level.

"Whew, I'll be happy for an iced frappe-whatever they make at that fancy coffee shop you like," Geraldine said, fanning herself with her wide brimmed hat before putting it on.

"That does sound good," Eva admitted. They took off toward the coffee shop, and Eva was thankful it wasn't too far. She would be happy to enjoy the shade of the shop's large front porch—and the fans.

"Tell me, Eva," Geraldine said, as they neared the coffee shop. "Do you really think the refuge will just give out that woman's information?"

Eva held open the door and they stepped inside, blessed coolness washing over them both. "I'm not sure," she admitted as they walked to the ordering station. "But I think it's the next best step."

"What about Jerome?" Geraldine said as the barista stepped forward.

The question made her stumble through her order, and she waited to answer until her friend had placed her order as well and paid for them both.

"What do you mean?" she asked as they stepped back

to wait for the coffees.

"I mean, have you talked with him? Do you know where he's at?"

Eva chuckled. "It's not like he keeps me informed," she said with a small smile.

"That's not completely true now, is it?" Geraldine pointed out. "He told you an awful lot that morning on the beach."

Eva remembered that she had shared with them at their last book club meeting, but she didn't see that as something he would continue to do. "I think he just happened to share some unimportant information. That's all."

Geraldine tilted her head to the side. "I don't think that's it at all."

"Oh?" Their orders came up and Eva carried them out to a shaded table with a lovely view of the ocean.

"The way I see it," Geraldine said, taking a sip of her blended coffee drink, "is that you're both working two sides of the same coin. Why wouldn't you want to compare notes?"

"It's not that simple."

"What's complicated about it?"

Eva paused, thinking about the point the woman was making. "Perhaps, the way I see it is we're looking into it as a book club—or, more accurately, a group of people who like to solve mysteries. Jerome is working at it from a detective's perspective."

"And never the two shall meet?" she asked.

"It's more like—never the two shall be on the same

page." Eva scrunched her nose in thought. "Not necessarily by choice but by convention."

"I see." Geraldine took another thoughtful sip. "I still think you should talk with him. He might surprise you."

"And what? Make me an honorary deputy?" She smiled at the mere thought.

"No. Don't be silly. But he might let you...oh, I don't know, freelance?"

"That doesn't happen."

"Doesn't it?"

Eva opened her mouth to protest, but she didn't actually know.

"All I'm saying..." Geraldine slurped another long draw on her coffee. "Look, you two make a good team and it would be better to work *together* than apart."

The topic changed as their coffees dwindled, but Geraldine's words sat heavy on Eva's mind. Unknown to Geraldine, her suggestion made Eva think of the past. The idea of sharing ideas with Jerome wasn't a foreign one. She wanted to share what she learned, but she did feel as if she were walking on eggshells around him with regards to the case. It was uncomfortable not knowing if he'd be frustrated that the book club had dug more deeply into a case than perhaps they should have.

Still, Geraldine had a good point. They really would benefit from sharing information—on both sides—and they'd likely put an end to retracing the steps of the other. If only they could agree on some sort of arrangement.

Was it too much to hope that she and Jerome could get along when it came to murder?

12

Eva was early. A full twenty minutes earlier than she'd anticipated since the walk took much less time than she'd thought it would. Either she'd picked up her pace or she hadn't read the clock correctly when she left for the coffee shop to meet Ruben.

She considered taking a walk along the row of shops yet to be opened, but the fragrant scent of breakfast coming from the café's open doors drew her inside. Her stomach rumbled and she wondered if Ruben would mind if she ordered early.

The inside of the café was quiet with soft music playing in the background. The menu was written on four large chalk boards above the counter and she stood there studying them, contemplating what she would get. Ruben had just mentioned coffee, but surely he wouldn't mind if she got breakfast before he arrived.

"I hear their omelets are the best."

She flinched at the deep voice coming behind her right

shoulder. When she turned, her surprise turned to pleasure. "What are you doing here, Jerome?" Her eyes flashed to the omelet, cup of fruit, and coffee on the tray he held.

"A detective's got to eat too, you know."

She laughed. "I do hear they are human."

"Unfortunately." He dipped his head in mock sorrow. "Are you here alone? Care to join me?"

His offer, so easily given, was tempting. She almost wanted to say yes for the next twenty minutes, perhaps talk to him about what Geraldine had mentioned, but Ruben was coming. It seemed unwise to sit with Jerome when she promised to meet with Ruben.

That thought alone was uncomfortable. It felt too much like commitment to Ruben—when she only viewed him as a friend. A good friend she went to coffee with, but a friend, nonetheless. Why should it matter who she had breakfast with?

"I see I've caught you off guard. Pretend I didn't say anything." He moved to walk past her, but she caught his arm, careful not to upset his tray.

"I'm meeting someone, but I could sit for a few minutes."

He held her gaze, and then his smile widened. "That'd be nice."

She ordered, taking his advice and getting a California omelet with avocado and turkey bacon, then joined him at his small table by the window. He wore a light blue shirt the color of the sky that day and jeans. Aside from seeing

136

him at the beach, this was the most relaxed she'd seen him.

After taking her first bite she let out a *mmmm*.

"Good?" he asked, taking a sip from his coffee.

"You were definitely right about the omelets."

He nodded as he took another bite. Chewing thoughtfully, he looked over at her.

"What?"

"Nothing," he said, swallowing and wiping his mouth with a napkin. "How have you been?"

She thought back to what Geraldine had said. Was it possible that she and Jerome could work together? She had a feeling that, as a detective, he wouldn't want to be bogged down by a group of crime-solving readers, but he probably would admit that they'd done well on the last two cases they'd worked on.

Instead she said, "I've been doing well. Things at the bed-and-breakfast are very busy right now."

"Oh?" He took another sip of his coffee.

Eva wished she'd gotten some, but her plan was to finish her breakfast with Jerome and then have the coffee while she spoke with Ruben. It felt a little odd sitting here and she couldn't help that her gaze kept traveling to the front door for a sign of when Ruben would come in. Then again, she was just having breakfast with a friend and coffee with another friend. That was all. Wasn't it?

"Yes," she said, bringing herself back to the present. "It seems we're either booked through the weekend or through the week, not much of a break in-between."

"Have you thought of expanding?"

She'd just taken another bite of her omelet and chewed as she considered his question. "I have," she said, when she'd swallowed, "but the time and the arrangement has never been right."

"How so?"

"I'd like to purchase someplace that is close—ideally next to or behind—my original property, but I don't think it'll happen. I know the neighbors to the left of us. They're great people and will be passing down their home to their children for a vacation rental. And the lot behind is owned by an older man who insists he has no desire to sell. I would never force someone so...it looks like a no-go."

"But what about elsewhere on the Key?" He seemed to be genuinely interested in expansion for her.

She smiled. "I can't really split myself in two, Jerome. How would that work?"

"Well, it stands to reason if you're booked now, you could also be booked elsewhere. Sure, it would take hiring someone to manage a second property, but I wouldn't let location stop you."

She bobbed her head from one side to the other. "That's a thought. I kind of like the personal touch I have at the Key's though. I'm the owner and caretaker, and often times that's why people come to B&B's—for the connection and the atmosphere."

"I see." Jerome looked thoughtful for a moment. "I didn't think about the connection you make with guests though. That makes sense. How's the photography going?"

He seemed to have no end of questions and she shared how she was taking photos for Elijah's art opening. He sounded excited at the opportunity for her.

There was a lull and her mind immediately filled it with questions about the case. She knew better than to ask them, but then she thought about Lilly. She and Geraldine were planning to go talk to the young woman after her coffee with Ruben, and she knew she should tell Jerome. And yet there was really nothing *to* tell.

There was a woman whose pen she'd found in a dead woman's apartment. They were both conservationists and had both been to the refuge. It stood to reason that a pen like that, something often given out all over, could be in Beth's possession.

It felt a little like she was justifying holding back information, but just as she thought she might give in and tell him her plans, Ruben walked in.

It was clear he was surprised to see her sitting with Jerome. His gaze took in their small table and breakfast dishes. Then he looked to Jerome, his eyes narrowing as he approached them.

She darted from her chair, tossing her napkin on the dregs of her omelet.

"There you are," she said, forcing a bright smile. "I got here early, and Detective Makos offered for me to join him until you arrived." Did it sound like she was making up an excuse to be eating breakfast with one man while promising to have coffee with the other? She hoped not.

"I see," Ruben said, his characteristic smile coming back, though not as brightly as normal.

"Hello, Ruben." Jerome stood up, moving her dishes to his tray, and then stacking the trays together. "Why don't you two take our table?"

"*Si*," Ruben said, nodding. "That would be nice. Thank you, Detective Makos."

"Please, call me Jerome," he said as the men shook hands.

"You two were not talking about something like a murder, were you?" Ruben asked. He added a chuckle, but she thought he was genuinely worried.

"Oh, no," Jerome laughed, and looked over at Eva. "Not this time."

For some reason his gaze made her stomach clench and her cheeks heat. Something about the familiarity they both had and how, if given the time, they likely *would* have talked about Beth Swanson's murder. And the reality was...she would have welcomed the topic.

"Well, I'll talk to you later," Jerome said, dipping his head toward Eva. "Good to see you, Ruben."

"Same," Ruben said, watching him as he tossed their trash, off-loaded their dishes to a plastic tub, and then stacked their trays.

She watched him leave and then remembered Ruben. "Coffee?"

"We could walk if you are full already," he offered.

"Not at all." She made sure she met his gaze. "I waited to have coffee with you. As you asked."

"Ah, *dulzura*, that is good."

They ordered their coffee and sat back down at the table she'd shared with Jerome. They talked about his trip to Cuba, which they still hadn't discussed since they'd both been so busy, and then he maneuvered the conversation to an outing he had in mind.

"I really think you would like it, Eva."

"A cabaret? I'm not sure." She didn't even like musicals, let alone singing and dancing and dinner. It sounded a little too busy for her tastes.

"They are amazing dancers, and the food is..." He kissed his fingers. "*Delicioso.*"

"Let me think about it?"

"What is to think about?" he said, leaning forward and gripping her hand. "It will be the best fun you've had in a long time. No boring books or frightful murders."

She wanted to argue that she never thought books were boring and murders were simply something to be solved, but she had a feeling Ruben wasn't in the mood to hear that.

"How about a deal," she said, nailing him with a look. "I go to the cabaret with you, and you finally show me designs for the White Room?"

He rolled his eyes. "If you insist."

"It's a deal then," she said.

"It's a date," he replied, taking her hand and kissing her knuckles.

Her mouth went dry, and she started to protest that it really wasn't a date, but he pushed away from the table. "I'm going to get a refill."

She checked her watch and saw that it was nearing the time she promised to stop by and pick up Geraldine. She stood and followed Ruben to the counter where he waited on his cup to be refilled with iced coffee.

Standing there with one hand in the pocket of his white linen pants, Eva couldn't help but notice his good looks. Once again, he wore a brightly colored shirt that showed off his personality. He was a few inches shorter than her but had a confidence that made him appear taller. Somehow bigger than life, or something like that.

She was certain that's how he'd gotten all of the contracts he had on the island. His construction business did well, and Eva wasn't surprised. He'd made sure to hire fellow Cubans who needed to send money home, along with other workers who got the job done fast and efficiently.

"I've got to get going," she said when he had his cup in hand.

"Can I drop you somewhere?" he asked.

"No, thanks." She followed him outside and saw his truck parked in a space halfway down the block. "I'm picking up Geraldine."

"All right. Well, I will call you about the cabaret. You'll love it," he said, kissing each of her cheeks as he started off toward his truck.

She watched him go and then ordered an Uber on her phone. The wait was ten minutes, so she searched out shade when she saw Jerome at a corner table on the outdoor patio space. He'd been watching her and Ruben.

"You're still here?" she said, joining him at his table in the shade.

"I'm still here," he agreed. "You don't look happy."

She blinked. She didn't? "I don't?"

"No. Something he said made your back go all stiff and those frown lines on your forehead say that you aren't pleased."

"Ah, right, you're a detective. Why are you 'detecting' me?" She laughed, and he smiled but didn't join the laughter. He looked serious. "To be honest, Ruben invited me to the cabaret."

"And that's a bad thing?"

"It is if you don't like musicals." She shuddered. "My mother loved them, but my father and I were the ones who liked to watch true crime documentaries or the news, of all things."

Now Jerome laughed. "The news?"

"I know. Not really a good comparison, but let's just say I don't like musicals or the cabaret."

"But you're going?"

She looked back to the space where Ruben's company truck had been. The space was empty now. "We made a deal."

"What kind of deal."

"He'll start the plans for renovating one of my rooms if I go with him. I suppose it's fair."

"I suppose." Jerome narrowed his eyes at her. "Would you go if it were something else?"

"I think it would depend," she said, chuckling. "Definitely not singing and dancing." She made a face.

"You are a constant surprise, Eva," he said just as her car pulled up.

She stood. "That's my ride. I've got to go pick up Geraldine."

"What are you two ladies up to?" he said, taking the last sip of his coffee.

She opened her mouth to answer then paused. And by the way Jerome looked at her, she wore a guilty expression.

"Spill the beans, Ms. Stewart."

"We're going to talk with Lilly Quinn."

He looked completely stunned, and it gave her a moment of happiness to shock the detective.

"Do you want to come with us?"

"You are a constant surprise, Ms. Stewart," he said, standing and tossing his cup in the trash. "Seeing as I'm off duty, I suppose I could come with you as a purely curious party."

"That's it? Do you promise not to take over our conversation?"

"You mean interrogation," he said, looking amused.

"Come on," she said, motioning him to the car. "We'll let Geraldine give you the ground rules. She's much better at this than I am."

They hopped into the car and headed to the older woman's home. When she slid in next to Eva who was next to Jerome, Geraldine did a double take.

"What is *he* doing here?"

Eva laughed and Jerome pretended to look wounded. "It's nice to see you too, Mrs. Walker."

"It's Geraldine and you are *not* getting in our way, sunny boy."

Eva could see he was trying hard not to break into laughter, but he was losing the battle so Eva rescued him. "I went to have coffee with Ruben today and Jerome was there."

"So, you ditched the contractor?" Geraldine said, adjusting her linen blouse and shifting the weight of her large handbag on her lap.

"What? No. I just stopped to have a bit of breakfast with Jerome before Ruben came and then—"

"Cut to the point, dearie." Geraldine's look made Eva realize she was rambling.

"He's coming with us."

"I can see that. But why?"

"Do I really need to get into what it is that I do for a living?" Jerome looked amused more than frustrated, something Eva was glad for.

"Oh, I know what you do," Geraldine said, leaning forward to look across Eva in the cramped backseat of the SUV. "Just not sure why you're doing it with us."

Jerome burst into a laugh and shook his head. "You do have some firecracker friends, Eva." He shook his head, leaning back in the seat which made his muscled shoulder rub against hers. "But to answer your question, Geraldine, I think it would be more accurate to say I'm *letting* you continue on with this meeting rather than stopping it so I can conduct it as the lead detective on the case."

"Hoity toity," Geraldine said, but Eva saw the crack of a smile on her lips. "I think we can agree to that."

Eva and Jerome shared a look and then the cab fell silent until they reached the Bay View Hotel and Spa. The driver pulled over and Eva thanked him, making sure to leave a tip via the phone app before climbing out.

Once they were on the sidewalk, she turned to face Jerome. "I was connected with Miss Quinn from the conservation agency she works with. I'm here under the guise of being an interested donor to her next project. Geraldine is coming as a friend, but truthfully, I'm worried you may be recognized."

"And you won't be?"

Eva shook her head. "No, I had my hair up and wore a hat at the refuge. I'm fairly certain I look much different than I did on the island."

She caught Jerome's appreciative glance at her sundress and sandals. She'd taken care to add more makeup and wear her hair down which, surprising as it may sound, made her look very different than she had on the day Beth's body had been found.

"Fair enough. I'll get a table and sit with my back to you, will that work?"

Eva agreed. It was a good solution, if they could find the right tables. She looked up as they approached the large hotel on the West Bay that overlooked the water. Palms lined the walkway to the expensive hotel and spa. The manicured lawn stretched all the way down to the water, and guests in luxury brand everything walked back and forth.

"Fancy place," Jerome said, looking around the lobby when they walked inside.

"They have a lobster tail roll that is to die for," Geraldine said. She indicated the restaurant attached to the hotel.

"I'm sure I couldn't afford it, not on my salary," Jerome said with a chuckle.

Eva walked up to the front desk and asked them to page Lilly Quinn. When she rejoined Jerome and Geraldine, they were talking about favorite restaurants.

"She's on her way down. I told her we'd meet her on the back patio."

The three of them walked out to the back patio that overlooked the water. It was stunning with a large pool area to the left, green grass flowing all the way to the small beach, and a large outdoor seating area with overhead bistro lights. There was no question this area would look just as good—if not better—at night.

They selected a set of tables in the shade near a fan. Eva sat facing the door to the back patio area so she could see Lilly, and Jerome sat directly behind her.

"Anyone else think it's odd she's staying here?" Jerome said, not turning around.

"Maybe the girl has money?" Geraldine said.

"Then why would she need Eva's donation?"

"Perhaps there's something about personal money and conservation money?" Eva mused. But she'd been thinking along the same lines as Jerome. Why would a woman like Lilly, who admittedly looked rugged in appearance at the island, be staying at one of the most expensive hotels in Key West?

Then Eva remembered the computer. "Did you find a link between Beth and Lilly?"

"No," Jerome said, sounding frustrated though she couldn't see his expression. "The only new development in the case is that the numbers on the note in Beth's hand did correspond to the location where her body was found."

Eva was about to turn around to hear more when she saw Lilly walk out. Eva almost did a double take. She wore a long white dress showing off a deep tan with expensive high-heeled sandals and an even more expensive purse hanging at her side. She looked nothing like the woman on the island with her odd bodyguard.

"She's coming," Eva said, then waved the woman over.

"You must be Eva?" Lilly said.

"Yes, thanks so much for meeting me. This is my friend, Geraldine."

"Lovely to meet you both. You look so familiar," Lilly said, and Eva heard Jerome cough behind her, but she remained composed.

"I've been told I have one of those faces. This hotel is amazing," Eva said, changing the subject.

"It's very nice," Lilly said, seeming to accept Eva's explanation, though she thought the woman looked a little uncomfortable. "Now, about the donation you were considering. What can I tell you that will help you make a decision to support the natural wildlife of Florida?"

"Perhaps you can tell me more about what you do." Eva asked.

Lilly obliged, talking in detail about her work with

newts in the area but also the other conservationists she'd worked with in Florida. Despite her wealthy appearance, the woman spoke like a true conservationist and her passion made it obvious that she cared a great deal about the nature in Key West.

"I've been doing a bit of research on my own," Eva said when there was a break in the conversation. "And I saw the article about the woman who died at the Great White Heron refuge. I didn't realize conservation work was dangerous."

"Oh," Lilly looked flustered. "I—I wouldn't say it's dangerous exactly…"

"Did you know the woman? Beth something?"

"Beth Swanson," Lilly said, then looked as if she wished she hadn't. "I—I did know Beth. We'd worked on a few projects together."

"Oh, I'm so sorry. What were you doing? Was it with newts?" Eva remembered the information she'd discovered about how valuable newts could be. Was it possible Lilly was smuggling them? But if so, how did Beth fit in?

"No." Lilly looked around as if she wanted the waiter they'd sent away to come back. "She was working on rare songbirds."

"On a refuge around here?" Eva asked.

"Yes." Lilly looked out toward the water, and Eva shared a look with Geraldine.

"Honey, you look preoccupied," Geraldine said, reaching out to rest a sunspotted hand on top of hers. "Is something the matter?"

"What? Oh, no." She pulled her hand back with a forced smile, and Eva glanced where the woman had been looking. The same burly man who had been at the refuge stood across the patio staring back at Lilly.

"Who's that? Your boyfriend?" Eva asked.

"Boyfriend? I—oh, no. That's Tim. He's...a friend." It was clear now that the woman was lying, though Eva was sure the man wasn't a boyfriend. He didn't seem to be a friend to her either.

"I'm sorry, can we maybe reschedule this?" Lilly asked.

"Is something wrong?" Geraldine asked again.

"I'm not feeling well."

Eva watched as two other men who looked similar to Tim joined him. Same build, same dark skin, same intense stare focused on Lilly.

"Um, I suppose so. I'm sorry you're feeling ill. Is there anything we can do?"

"No." Lilly stood up, her chair clattering back.

Eva felt Jerome shift behind her, but she reached out to steady the chair and said, "It's all right." While it looked like she was talking to Lilly, she was actually saying it to Jerome.

"I'll be in touch," she said as Lilly practically ran from the patio.

They sat still watching as Tim and his buddies walked through the patio inside the way Lilly had gone.

"Coast clear?" Jerome asked.

"Yes," Eva said, standing quickly, "but I think we need to follow those men."

"Men? What men?"

"Come on, detective," Geraldine said, "take me for a promenade."

He shot a helpless look at Eva who smiled and then motioned for them all to go inside. Once their eyes adjusted to the dim lighting, Eva's spirits fell. There was no sign of Tim or the men who had been with him. The lobby was empty and so were her chances of finding out who Tim really was.

13

BACK AT THE POLICE STATION, after dropping Geraldine off, Jerome questioned Eva—yet again—about Tim.

"You spoke with him on the island, or someone did. I don't think I can tell you much more than what they found out," she insisted.

"Is it possible he recognized you?" he asked.

"Maybe he recognized you."

They held each other's gaze for a moment longer before Jerome let out a sigh and shuffled papers across his desk.

"I think it was Officer Kent who took the statements of the witnesses, but he doesn't note much about Tim Mantel and Lilly Quinn. They claimed to be dating and out enjoying an afternoon at the refuge."

"That's clearly false."

"What?" He looked up from the folder in his hand.

"The way that Lilly looked at Tim was nothing like a

woman who's seen the man she's dating. It was a look filled with fear, not attraction."

"I can't arrest someone on the grounds that the woman they're supposed to be dating looked afraid of them."

"Of course not," Eva said, refolding her arms across her chest in the chilly police station bullpen. "But I'm assuming a check on Tim Mantel has been done?"

"Actually…" Jerome made a face the looked like he'd bitten into a lemon. "Seems like Kent hasn't put through any additional requests. What is going on around here?" He shuffled through more paperwork. "I'll run his and Lilly's identification and see what comes up. In the meantime, please stay away from Lilly and her maybe-boyfriend. If there were 'goons' with him, as Geraldine said, then I definitely don't want you to be anywhere near them."

Warmth from his concern flooded her chest, but she laughed it off. "I don't think they're interested in *me* so much as in Lilly. There's a connection here that I'm missing."

"We're missing," he said, giving her a pointed look.

She dipped her head in acquiescence.

"Eva, do you think Lilly or Tim is responsible for Beth's death?"

"I can't say about Tim," she said, "but Lilly seemed to be truly sad that her friend was dead, if not a little hesitance."

"As in a hesitation that comes with guilt?"

"It didn't appear that way to me, but you can never truly know, can you?"

"I suppose not." He leaned back in his chair. "I'll look into them and have Kent call them in for a 'routine' conversation about the murder. It will give me a chance to talk with her and see how her story holds up to what she told you."

"Do you think Tim will show?"

"I have no way of knowing. But we'll see."

Eva nodded and stood. "I need to get back to the Key's. I promised to help Anton with some preparations for the weekend."

Jerome sat up. "Is it about the brunch thing?"

"Brunch...thing?"

Jerome held up his hands. "I'll admit to a little snooping. I saw Anton at the grocery store last Saturday and—"

"He told you about our plans."

"In great, excited detail."

She laughed. "I think he's told half the island about our idea. I don't think there's any way I can stop it now."

"You want to stop it?"

Eva shrugged. "It's like when you asked me about plans to expand the B&B. I like the idea of expansion and I like the idea of brunch, but I don't like the possible risk that comes along with it. Like booking out the room or making sure my guests don't feel overlooked by me allowing outsiders to come for breakfast. Things like that."

As if he didn't realize what he was doing, Jerome

reached out and took her hand, squeezing it gently. "I think it's a great idea and I'm fairly certain your guests aren't going to mind one bit that you've got a mind for business." He quickly released her hand with a shy smile before turning back to his computer.

"Thanks, Jerome." She turned to go but paused to look back. "You just want to be on our opening list, don't you?"

He grinned up at her. "I wouldn't say no."

"Noted," she said, leaving his desk and heading to the lobby. She paused before exiting, deciding to stop by and see Vicky on a whim. She took the stairs rather than the elevator and exited into the even cooler space of the medical examiner's area.

"Vicky?" she called out, not sure if she would be working on an autopsy. If so, Eva would leave immediately—there was nothing there that she would want to see. She shivered just thinking about it.

"Eva?" Vicky popped her head out of her office and her smile blossomed. "Well, I'll be. It's good to see you here."

"You too," she said, giving the woman a quick hug.

"What are you up to?"

"I was with Jerome." Vicky's eyes flashed at this. "Just talking about the case," Eva added quickly.

"The case, hm?" Vicky wiggled her eyebrows.

"Oh stop." She shook her head.

"Stop what, darlin'?" Vicky laughed and tugged Eva into her office. "Just tell me, is there something there?"

"Something…with Jerome?" Eva dropped her voice.

"Well yeah, that's who you were meetin' right?"

"There is *nothing* there. We're just…friends." She said it

and wanted it to be true, even though applying the word to the handsome detective seemed a little premature. "Or I hope we will be someday."

"You've solved two cases together. I think that could constitute friendship."

"He solved them, I just happened to point him in the right direction a few times."

Vicky rolled her eyes and laughed. "I'm glad you're here though. I was going to call you after work. I need help picking out a dress for Elijah's opening."

"You're buying one?" Eva asked.

"Well, of course I am! It's a special occasion."

"I'm sure you have five dresses that would work."

"Oh, go on," she gently shoved Eva's shoulder, then pulled her to her computer. "I've narrowed in on these three."

On Vicky's screen were three images of dresses lined up side by side. One was short, red and went off both shoulders. The other was black and tight down to just above the knee. The third was a rich emerald color. It was fitted through the waist and then went out into a semi-full skirt"

"Wow, those are all beautiful."

"I know." Vicky let out a sigh. "I can't decide. I like them all."

If it had been anyone else Eva would have joked that she buy them all, but she had a feeling the woman might take her up on it.

"What do you think?" Vicky asked.

Eva studied the images again and her eye continued to

come back to the red dress. It was a bold choice, but she felt like it would be most appropriate in the gallery and would match Vicky best.

"Red. Go with the red one."

"Really?" She looked up at Eva with a glow in her eyes. "I was thinking that one but didn't know if it was too bold."

Eva studied her friend for a moment. "You'll wear it well."

"Done," Vicky said, clicking on a link that brought her to a website of a dress shop in Miami. "It'll be here in a few days. I can't wait!"

Eva held her friend's gaze.

"What?" Vicky said, turning away from her computer.

"Have you talked with Elijah?"

"About...?"

"About the dinner invitation?"

"Oh, that." She bit her lip and looked back at the screen. "No. I just figured he's got enough on his plate as it is."

Eva frowned. She wanted to bring up the fact that Vicky could be giving the man the wrong idea—that dress would certainly speak for itself—but then she recalled how she wasn't keen on discussing the men in her life, friend or not.

"All right then."

"All right?"

"I trust your judgment," Eva said with a smile.

Vicky looked like she though Eva was joking, then shrugged. "All right."

"Well, I'm glad I stopped by," Eva said. "I've got to get going. I'm helping Anton this afternoon and then Elijah tonight."

Vicky nodded. "I was going to go and help with the gallery tonight too. Unfortunately, there are some results needed by tonight, so I won't be able to make it. Tell everyone I'm there in spirit."

Eva laughed. "Will do. And I'll go so you can get back to work."

"I was on my lunch break," Vicky said, following her to the door, "but I do have quite a bit to get done. I'll see you Friday at *La Bella*?"

"Yes. Looking forward to ravioli."

"It's all about their cheesy parmesan bread for me," Vicky laughed. "But I'll have to go easy. Got to fit into that dress!"

They said their goodbyes and Eva ascended to the main lobby and then out to the street where she hailed a cab. Once inside and making her way back to the bed-and-breakfast, she considered what Lilly had told her. She had seemed genuinely excited about her conservationist work, and yet there had been real fear in her eyes when she caught sight of Tim. There was clearly something else going on, but Eva couldn't be certain.

The main thing they had to figure out was who had gained the most from Beth's death. From where she sat now, *no one* had gained anything. Other than a senseless killing, which Eva didn't think was possible. There had to be a reason for the woman's death. She just had to find it.

"THIS IS STARTING to look like a real art gallery," Eva said, standing in the middle of the modern section and doing a slow twirl.

"You think so?" Elijah asked, looking around the gallery as she did.

"I do." She paced to the back and then moved to the impressionist side. "Everything looks incredible Elijah."

"You had a lot to do with it," he said with a chuckle. "Thank you for your help."

They had been working for over an hour setting up the lighting so that it best represented each piece. It was something the gallery had offered to do for Elijah after they hung his paintings, but he'd opted to do it himself.

He'd asked Eva to come and help him, but she'd questioned him as to *why* he wanted her. His explanation had left her slightly teary-eyed. He'd explained that as a photographer, she had to think about lighting and he wanted her eye to be able to judge if he'd done each painting correctly.

Willard had planned to be there as well, but Bonnie had forgotten to tell him about a party they were invited to, so it had ended up being just Eva and Elijah. They'd done quick work and she felt as if everything was ready.

"I think it was really your work and I just gave an opinion, but you are very welcome."

He tossed a hand at her as if to stave off her compliment. Then he spun to the front.

"Oh no," he said.

"What is it?"

"I totally forgot the front windows."

She turned to the front and saw darkness, though there was artwork set up. Since it was night and the sun had set, the blinds were already closed so no one would see the work until opening night. In the meantime, they had to make sure when the blinds were raised, the artwork was lighted well.

"Let's do it really quickly," she suggested.

"Are you sure? It's getting late."

"It's only nearing ten, and I promise I won't turn into a pumpkin."

He grinned and then agreed.

They both rushed to the front, and he started maneuvering the lights around to highlight his pieces in the best way. Not too much shine on the art varnish and not too close or else the light would wash out the art itself. Thankfully none of his pieces were under glass so the reflections were not an issue.

Finally, twenty minutes later, they finished the windows. "I think that's it," he said, nudging the last light over a few millimeters.

"Great," Eva smiled. "I'll go outside and let you know how it looks. Can you raise the curtains?"

"I think so," he said looking at the complex pulley system. "Give me a minute?"

She nodded and stepped outside. Immediately, the humidity of the air wrapped around her like a warm, but slightly damp blanket. She didn't mind it though since the gallery was air-conditioned and she'd started to feel somewhat cold.

The sounds of nightlife a few blocks away floated over to her. It was a weekday and yet that didn't stop vacationers from enjoying the many nightclubs and nightlife attractions Key West had to offer.

She turned around to look at the window, but it was still covered. Elijah was clearly having trouble with raising the blinds. She took a few steps back into the street. There was no traffic, since this street had little to offer in the way of adventure and fun.

Her eyes started to adjust to the darkness and just as she was about to go back in to see if he needed help, she heard a shuffling sound behind her. Spinning around, her eyes took in the dark shapes of the shops and lush vegetation, but nothing else.

A cat darted across her path, startling her back just as the brightness from the front window increased. She turned to see Elijah had the blinds up and she began studying the placement of the lights.

Another shuffling sound came from behind her, but when she turned there was nothing there again. She was letting the darkness get to her. Instead, she focused on instructing Elijah to move a few of the lights just slightly for the best placement and she gave him a thumbs-up. Moments later, he dropped the curtain and the street grew dark again.

She pushed the door open, but Elijah met her there with her purse just as the lights went out, shrouding them in darkness. The only light was a streetlamp nearly a block away.

"Oh, that's dark," she said, accepting her purse.

"Sorry." He laughed as he locked the door. "I figured you'd want to get out of here now that we're done, but I didn't think about the darkness."

"No, it's all right." She still felt uneasy from the sounds she'd heard before. Was it possible a homeless person was across the street settling in for the night?

"Let's walk over to Southernmost Bar. We'll have a better chance of hailing a cab there."

"All right," she said, looking behind them. Nothing was there.

They fell into step with only the silence of the night around them, but Eva's mind was on the sounds. She knew better than to frighten herself, but she was also adept at sensing when something wasn't quite right.

A scuffle behind them made her stomach tense. She grabbed Elijah's arm and gave it a squeeze. "It's such a nice night," she said loudly, squeezing his arm again.

"What's wrong?" he asked in a whisper.

"I think someone is following us. Do you have your phone?"

"Yes."

He pulled it out and she instructed him to call the police, using the non-emergency line. It was possible they had a police car in the area that could drive by.

Then, as quickly as she dared, she turned around, still holding Elijah's arm. There was a man a block away walking behind them. He was clearly following them, but she didn't know if that was pure happenstance or by choice.

Elijah talked on the phone quietly, and they picked up their pace. They still had several blocks to go before they reached the street where the bar was located, and now it looked as if the man had sped up as well.

They pushed their speed a little more as Elijah stayed on the phone, likely something the operator had instructed, and Eva risked another glance.

Somehow, her timing caught the man directly under a dim streetlamp. He had dark hair that hung to his shoulders and a solidly built frame with muscled arms pulling his shirt tight across his shoulders. She couldn't be completely certain, but it looked like one of the men—the goons as Geraldine had called them—from the hotel and her meeting with Lilly.

"We have to hurry, Elijah," she said, panic slipping past her naturally calm exterior.

"Okay," he said, speeding up to match her pace.

She glanced back again and was dismayed to see the man had gained on them. They were just one block away from bright lights, but at this pace, the man was going to overtake them. Eva was considering contingency plans like screaming loudly when a police car rounded the corner up ahead and flashed its lights.

Eva breathed out a sigh of relief as the car came to stop next to them. They explained that they had been the ones to call, and when she looked back, the man was gone.

The officer, a nice man named Josh, offered them both a ride home and they accepted. After dropping Elijah off,

Eva got out at the bed-and-breakfast and thanked the man again. He told her to be careful and even waited to leave until she was safely inside.

Her breaths came in sharp gasps as the reality of their situation finally caught up with her, but she quickly calmed down. Perhaps it had just been her imagination, but either way she was glad to be home. After double-checking that the B&B doors were locked, she made her way to her cottage—rushing despite how foolish she felt—and locked herself safely inside.

Fifteen minutes later, with a cup of hot tea and a book in hand, she settled on the couch to calm down. The quiet was short-lived when a knock shattered the silence.

"Eva? It's Jerome. Open up."

14

Eva checked the clock, surprised to see it was just after eleven, but she went to the door and, after checking through the peep hole, opened the door.

"Jerome? What are you doing here? It's late."

"I know but—can I come in?"

"Of course." She stepped back and he came in, pulling off the baseball cap he wore. He was dressed in slacks and a nice button up shirt with a jacket over top that he was now pulling off. She almost smiled to see his tie askew around his neck. It looked like he'd come straight from the office, though he must have gone home to change after she'd left him earlier that day.

She closed the door. "What's going on?"

"I wanted to ask you the same thing," he said, tossing his jacket and cap on the bench by the door. "I heard your name motioned in a report about suspicious activity over by the art gallery. Talked to Roth—'er Josh—and he told me what happened. Are you all right?"

His concern was palpable and she took a step back, somehow unable to think with him so close. "I—please. Sit down. Do you want some tea?"

"Tea? You're offering me tea when you were *followed* tonight?"

"I'm fine," she said, meeting his gaze. "And I'll tell you all about it, but please come sit. How about some tea? The water's hot."

He nodded. She poured him a cup of chamomile tea and then joined him on the couch.

"Now tell me everything," he said, taking a sip and placing the cup on the coffee table.

"There's not much to tell really," she said, taking a sip of her own tea. "I was helping Elijah at the gallery and when we went to walk to a bar a few blocks away to grab a cab, I noticed someone was following us."

"And you're certain they were following *you*."

"Yes. I mean, at first I wondered, but as they got closer..." She cut the admission off. Did she really want to make the claim that it was one of the men with Tim?

"What?"

"The man looked like one of the men with Tim at the hotel."

Jerome set his mug down with a clang. "Are you sure?"

"That's why I was hesitant to say—I'm not positive. I'm fairly certain it was the man standing to his right as we looked over at Tim, but I can't be fully sure since he was at least a block away the whole time."

Jerome rubbed a hand across his forehead, and it was only then that Eva realized he looked tired. *Very* tired.

"Are you all right?" she asked.

He barked out a laugh. "You are asking me if I'm all right? Eva…." He shook his head as if he couldn't believe it.

"Well, you look tired."

"I am. But mostly I'm tired of having no idea who killed Beth Swanson." His admission hung in the air between them, and Eva reached over to squeeze his hand. The contact surprised him, but he didn't pull away.

"It's because there seems to be no motive."

"True. We're still looking into her past and her computer, but forensically there's nothing to tie a killer to her. There were no fingerprints on the note or the strap, so they were obviously wearing gloves, and though the strap from the camera was the weapon used to strangle her, there is nothing else. No evidence of the camera that accompanied the strap. We assume the killer took it with him or tossed it into the water, but we don't know."

"No boot prints?"

"No. I mean, there were a few but they were matched to the victim, Darnell Forrester, Casey Ferrington, and the fish and wildlife officer Paul Hart." At Eva's look he explained, "Officer Hart said that he'd been out there that morning to check on the area. Something about it being a special mating section for the Great White Heron."

"I saw the sign for no entry."

"Apparently, he'd just put it up." Jerome ran a hand over his face. "And then Beth was there, but the refuge organizer said they had no record of her working there officially."

"She was visiting?"

"That's what they say—not sure if they're trying to cover themselves from bad press—but it doesn't seem to fit with her nature."

"You mean how passionate she was about conservation."

"Yes, and—"

"Wait." Eva sat up straighter. Something Kay had said came back to her.

"What is it?"

"I should have told you this before," she said, sending him a sheepish look.

"Go on." He didn't look mad, just interested.

"My friend, Kay—the dog groomer. She has a conservationist friend who works all over Florida. She said that Beth had come here to work at the refuge. Perhaps we had the wrong refuge? But in addition to that, she was looking into rumors of smuggling."

"Smuggling what?"

"That was Geraldine's question—"

"Does everyone in your murder book club know about this except for me?" Jerome still didn't look angry, just put out.

"I'm sorry." Eva shrugged. "I know you don't like us looking into your cases, but with Vicky and I practically finding this case for you…"

"Just tell me what you found out." He shook his head, rubbing again at the bridge of his nose.

"We were told that there are lots of valuable animals in Key West that people will pay money for. Apparently, smuggling is quite a big deal down here. Perhaps you haven't run across it yet since you've only been here a few months." He shrugged and she went on. "In the limited research I did, I did find that there are certain newts that can fetch a high price."

"Newts as in—Lilly Quinn the newt expert?"

"That's what I'm thinking, yes. It's another reason why I wanted to talk with her, but it could explain Tim and his buddies."

"How so?"

"If they're the smugglers, then maybe she works to find them the newts and they smuggle them out of the country—say to South America where they can fetch a high price."

"And what about Beth? She stumbled onto the whole thing?"

"It's possible." Eva let out a breath. "It would make sense why Lilly and Tim were on the island that day and why she had a paper with the location on it."

"Smuggling in broad daylight?" Jerome looked unconvinced.

"We won't know unless we find Tim and his friends."

"*We* won't be doing any of that. I've scheduled a cruiser to drive by at intervals tonight and you aren't to go anywhere without someone for the next few days." He pushed to the edge of the couch. "If Tim and his compatriots even *think* you're on to them, they won't stop at threatening you, Eva. You're in danger."

"But I'm not. I can't be." She shook her head. "They

only saw me meeting with Lilly, and if they ask her, she'll say I was an interested donor."

"Unless Tim recognized you. They had plenty of time to talk to her and don't forget—someone followed you."

Eva opened her mouth to say something, but Jerome interrupted.

"Just be careful."

"I will. I promise. I'm just going to dinner with the club and that's all."

He narrowed his eyes but then nodded. "You'll take a cab from here? And make sure someone walks you out to the cab you'll take home?"

"Scouts honor," she said, raising her fingers.

He smiled and then pushed to his feet. "I don't like you poking into cases," he said as he walked to pick up his hat and coat. "But I will admit, you and that club are helpful."

"Does that mean—"

"Nope." He held up a hand. "Don't press your luck. If you discover anything else, please let me know."

"Only if you tell me who Tim really is when you find out."

They stared each other down for almost a minute and then he broke into a slanted smile. "Fine."

"Deal."

She watched him take the path to the side of the bed-and-breakfast and then closed and locked the door. It was kind of him to stop by. The simple action made her feel cared for, in a friendly way, of course. It was strange how her deal with him left her feeling hopeful, whereas her deal with Ruben only made her dread her end of the bargain—namely the cabaret. He'd tried to get her to go with him that Friday, but she'd insisted the book club took precedence.

She walked back to the couch and sat, glancing toward Jerome's half empty mug of tea. She wasn't sure how she felt about his ultimatum to remain at the B&B, but she didn't plan to go anywhere. Still, she was independent, and the idea hurt her sensibility.

At the end of it all, only Jerome's kindness remained, and her ruffled feathers smoothed out at the thought.

GLASSES CLINKED and the scent of spicy Italian meatballs and pasta sauce filled the side room at *La Bella*. Conversation had been stilted by the presence of the waitstaff, but they were wrapping up their family style meal and would soon have the room to themselves.

"Where's that tiramisu?" Willard asked from his seat next to Elijah at the opposite end of the table to Eva.

"I canceled it. Thought you wouldn't want it—the diet and all," Elijah said, just managing to keep a straight face.

"You what?!"

"I'm kidding, I'm kidding," he said, laughing and patting Willard on the shoulder. "See? There's the waitress with the desserts."

They all got slices of tiramisu cake, and when the rest of their plates were cleared, Eva started by filling them in on what she'd learned from her meeting with Lilly. She also told them about her chat with Jerome. She did, however, leave out the fact that Jerome had come by to see her. No need adding to the ammo Vicky had already collected against her.

She knew her friend was harmlessly teasing her, but it was still an awkward subject. Her feelings for Jerome were of a professional nature and...well, perhaps not simply *professional*. She did like talking about photography with him, and she had really enjoyed their breakfast together but—

"Eva?"

She'd zoned out. "Sorry. I was just saying that I'm fairly certain the connection here is with smuggling, but I can't quite figure out *how* it all fits together."

"So, Lilly is helping Tim and his goons." Pete sent a look to Geraldine who had insisted that's what they should be called. "And Beth happened to get too close to their operation?"

"It would seem that way," Eva said. "Though it will be difficult to pull that together since there is really no physical evidence.

"But you can't just kill someone and not leave something behind." Willard looked around the table, eyeing the half-eaten cake Kay had left.

"No, no you can't." Eva admitted it didn't make sense. Either the killer wiped away their footprints or...well, there was no other option.

"Do we know who Tim really is yet?" Elijah asked, shoving the rest of his cake toward Willard who grinned and dug in.

"No. And that's a call I'm still waiting on."

"I know Jerome got hit with another case yesterday, so I've got a feeling he's swamped," Vicky said. She sat next to Kay who sat next to Pete. They all looked as flummoxed as Eva.

"The only thing to do is wait, I suppose." Eva poked at what was left of her cake.

"I don't like the sound of that," Geraldine said. "I mean, are we just going to let those little newts be shipped off to God knows where?"

Elijah coughed to cover a laugh, and Eva saw Vicky shoot him an amused look.

"How do they even smuggle something like that out of a refuge?" Pete asked.

"Pockets?" Willard said, making a motion to Eva about her cake.

She shot him down with a look, and then shook her head. "That seems unlikely. Wouldn't they just crawl out?"

The table dissolved into conversation about how a newt might be caught and smuggled, but Eva let her thoughts wander. Beth had to have prior knowledge about the smuggling. She'd been at the right place at the right time, but she assumed that Jerome hadn't found any communication about that on her computer. So how was she making these connections?

Her pocket started vibrating and she pulled out her phone. Jerome was calling.

"I'll be right back," she said to the table, then answered the phone as she exited the restaurant onto the back patio that overlooked the water.

"Hello?"

"Eva. I've got news."

"All right," she said, curious what he would tell her.

"Oh, did I get you at your dinner?"

"It's all right. I'm out the back while they haggle about smuggling newts."

"Um…" He sounded confused.

"Never mind."

"I finally got word back from my South American contact."

"About Tim?"

"Yes. And get this, it's not about newts, it's about songbirds."

Eva frowned. "Songbirds?"

"Yes! Apparently, they fetch a good price down here and the supply is abundant on many of the Keys in Florida. Tim, whose real name is Luis, is well known in the bird trade and auction business."

"Then why is he working with Lilly?"

"The best I can figure is that it has something to do with her access. He needed to be on that island in order to capture the birds."

"How does that work?" Eva could only imagine a man with a cage and that didn't line up with what they'd found.

"They have these specialized belts that wrap around their middle, under their shirts. The birds are small and fit in the capsules attached to the belt."

She thought back to the man's overly loose shirt. It was beginning to make sense.

"So…what? They were stealing birds and Beth

somehow got word of their meeting? But you found no evidence of Tim—Luis—being at the scene."

"I know. I have enough to bring him in, but of course now he's nowhere to be found. Lilly is in the wind as well, but we've got a BOLO out on her. I hope to have her found by tomorrow, but we'll see."

Eva thought back to the scene and how Lilly and Tim had looked. Nervous, yes, but did they have the faces of killers? Then again, Tim was a hard man to read. If he felt his operation had been threatened, he might consider murder. He had sent a man after her, hadn't he? Or had he?

Her memory tried to fill in details of the man from the night before, but the edges were fuzzy. Was it possible her imagination had conjured a man following her? The mind certainly could play games.

And if Tim—*Luis*—hadn't sent the man, and he wasn't concerned with her speaking to Lilly, then there could be other players could there be in this scheme.

She replayed what had happened the day of the murder. Walking along the path, taking photos, seeing a shape running through the trees, finding the body and Darnell finally admitting he'd known Beth. There was a possible connection—could he have known about the smuggling?

But more than that, the lack of evidence worried her the most. If footprints were only left by Beth, Darnell, Paul, and Casey—

"You still there?" Jerome said.

175

"Yes. Sorry. I was thinking." She rolled the new idea over in her mind. "What if we have this all wrong?"

"What do you mean?"

"Let me do some research, and then could we go out to the island tomorrow?"

"Eva, you need to tell me what you have."

"I don't *have* anything, but I do have an idea."

"Then tell me the idea."

And here it was. Their familiar crossroads.

"Listen, Jerome…" She shifted her weight and took a fortifying breath. "If I'm right—and you let me do my research first—will you agree to let the MMBC consult on some of your future cases?"

"Uh…" Jerome blew out a breath.

This was a big ask, she knew that, but what Geraldine had said came back to her. They were better off working together, weren't they? It was one thing for him to do the police work—that was obvious. But the possibility of helping with some of the details—some of the sleuthing—was too much to pass up.

"How about this," he said, countering her offer. "I let you do your research, assuming this is in-home research?"

"Yes," she said when he waited for an answer.

"And *if* things pan out the way you think, I'll consider consultation—but only with you."

"But—"

"I won't care whether you check in with your book club—making sure to keep confidential things confidential, of course. But if you get me this case, we'll have a deal."

She thought about countering his counter but assumed this was the best he was going to be able to do.

"Okay."

"Good."

He hung up and she returned to the dinner party only to make an excuse to go home. She had research to do, and a killer to catch.

15

"I CAN'T BELIEVE I'm going back out here," Jerome said, piloting the Key West PD's boat across the smooth, crystal clear waters of the Turkey Basin. "Will you tell me what you found *now?*"

"Not yet."

Eva sat back in her seat, the wind whipping her hair about her face as she enjoyed the ride. Her research, though not extensive, had confirmed a few things for her. A few very important things. She only hoped that she would be able to prove what she assumed had happened.

It would be in the explanation of things that the murderer would be revealed, but if they didn't confess, there was not much more that she could do. Though, she had a feeling forensics would be able to pull much more than she had already, and that thought comforted her.

The Great White Heron National Wildlife Refuge on the Johnston Key came into view and Eva forced her shoulders to relax. Jerome pulled the boat up to the dock, and after securing it, they climbed out.

"Follow me." She hadn't brought her camera today, and while she appreciated not having the extra weight, she was somewhat sorry since the clouds were out in a beautiful display of puffy white perfection.

"Talk," Jerome said, as they took the now familiar trail she and Vicky had taken.

"First off, thank you for humoring me. I know it's all very...cloak and dagger." She looked around. "Or maybe it's nature and trails, but I promise you this is more than a hunch for me. At least, I'm fairly certain that is true."

"You have good instincts," Jerome said, stepping over a downed log. "But my patience is wearing thin."

Then, up ahead at the dock that she had taken out over the water to photograph the scenery, they saw Paul Hart, the Federal Fish and Wildlife Officer on the refuge.

"What's Paul doing here?" he said to her.

"You'll see."

They approached him and she thanked him for coming. "I was wondering if you might clear up a few things for us, Paul." She continued down the trail toward the place where Beth had been murdered.

"Uh, sure. What can I help you folks with? Do you have new information about the body they found here?"

"We do," she said, feeling rather than seeing the glare Jerome sent her way. "But first, can you tell us why there was a sign here?" She pointed to the area where the Keep Out sign had been on the day of Beth's murder.

"I, uh…" He looked around, scratching at the back of his head. "It's mating season and—"

"But that's not true, is it Paul?" She caught the slight narrowing of Jerome's eyes. "I went on the refuge website, and it clearly states that breeding happens in March and April. Not July."

"Well…" He cleared his throat again. "Maybe they told me to put it up by accident."

"Because it's gone now," she said, pointing to the area again.

"And another question…" This time she turned to face him, noticing that Jerome looked more alert—possibly due to the fact that the officer had a gun at his belt. "This one is more personal. I noticed through Facebook that your daughter is going to Dartmouth. Is that correct?"

"I…yeah. How'd you know that?"

"Social media links to everything. But I'm curious to know how you and your wife—a stay-at-home mom to your other two daughters—how can you afford such an expensive school? And the private school your younger girls go to."

"Hey now—" he began, but Eva continued.

"And also, I talked with the station attendant before we left, and he pointed out your car in the park and boat lot —is it a Range Rover?"

He pressed his lips closed now, not responding to her jabs at his financial status.

"Believe me, Mr. Hart, I don't like to accuse anyone, but the facts are clear—*your* footprints were in an area where you didn't need to be. That's really the only true evidence we have in regard to Beth's murder. I'm sure if Detective Makos looks into your email communication, there will be no record of a request for a Keep Out sign in this area…which means you had no reason to be here. Unless it was to kill Beth Swanson."

"What do you have to say to that?" Jerome asked.

Paul remained silent.

"The thing is, Mr. Hart," Eva continued, wanting to show him all the evidence outright. "There is a smuggling operation on this very Key, and the only way that it would be possible is if someone was working on the inside. I'm sure this will all be corroborated by your bank statements, but what I don't understand is why Beth had to die."

Eva shook her head and continued. "Using your gloved hands, you put her camera strap around her throat and strangled her. I'm not sure what you thought would happen—wildlife would take care of the body perhaps? But then Darnell and Casey came upon the body and your plans went awry. Yet you didn't say anything, you let her death be a mystery. And that, I can't understand."

He clenched his jaw tightly and turned to face Jerome. "You gonna arrest me or what?"

"Is that a confession?" he asked, pulling out handcuffs.

"Read me my rights," was all he said.

EVA NURSED an iced tea and lime on the back porch as the fans blew warm air around her. Her bare feet were up on the railing, and she had a bowl of corn chips and salsa next to her, but her mind was elsewhere.

Jerome hadn't said much to her after arresting Paul Hart, but that was to be expected. He'd immediately gotten on the phone to call for backup, not that Paul had resisted, but it was protocol.

On reflection, she should have told Jerome everything *before* she took him to a meeting she'd arranged with a murderer, but she'd always had a bit of the flair for dramatics. And they'd had a wager, which made it feel important to make a show of what she'd discovered, so it had seemed the right choice. Only time would tell if that were true.

Still, now that she was home and safe, it was catching up with her. The long hours she'd spent on Facebook and Instagram scouring for information on Paul's family. She'd known he was local, and it was shockingly easy to find his wife's account. It was a public account that had listed his girls' accomplishments such as Dartmouth and their sports endeavors at their private school, the most expensive on the Key.

After a little distraction of Jerome at the docks to confirm which car was Paul's, she'd known without a doubt that he was the killer. It all came back to the footprints. A killer could have easily wiped prints away, but that would have taken *all* of the prints. Instead, they'd been left, and it was a clear indication of only three possibilities.

Darnell had no motive. His relationship with Beth had ended poorly, but he hadn't seen her in months. Casey had been cleared as well, since his injury made it impossible. That left the owner of the last set of prints —Paul.

And what better situation to help smugglers than the wildlife officer in charge of the refuge? He could easily have roped off certain areas of the island for 'conservation' issues, while secretly allowing smugglers free range. With Beth's investigation, Eva assumed she'd come across the details of the next meeting—explaining Lilly and Tim's presence on the island—and written herself a note. Then she'd brought her camera to capture the smugglers in the act, but that had been her downfall.

Eva only wondered what she'd been hoping to accomplish by keeping it secret. It made her sick to her stomach to think of all the birds that had been taken due to the fact Paul had been easily bought off. Of course, money was a powerful incentive. If only Beth would have reached out to the authorities first.

She was just about to close her eyes, thinking a nap might help, when Jake burst through the back door and pushed through the white curtains that cordoned off her special porch area.

"Jake, what's wrong?"

"Not wrong. *Right.*"

"Um, all right." She sat up, her feet landing softly on the rug. "What is it?"

"Well…" He took a chair and pulled it closer to her. "It was tough. A lot harder than I'd expected." He went into detail about how his professor had to help him and how they'd traced it through several different IP addresses, but finally she held up a hand.

"Cut to the point, Jake." She smiled so he'd know she wasn't angry, just confused.

"Right. Sorry." He pulled out a paper. "Do you know this person?"

Eva held up the paper and blinked to make sure she was seeing the name correctly. "This? This is who was emailing me?"

He nodded. "Do you know them?"

She shook her head. It was a white lie, but it was necessary. "Thank you for all your hard work. There'll be a bonus in your next check."

"You don't have to do that."

"I do," she said, smiling back at him. "You're not some errand boy doing anything I ask. This was a favor and I appreciate it."

"Are you...going to reply?" he asked.

"No." This time that was the truth.

"All right. Then I guess I'll toss this—"

"I'll take it." She held out her hand for the details. "Just in case they email me again. I can let them know I'm not interested."

His eyes narrowed and she didn't blame him. It did sound slightly suspicious, but then he shrugged and handed the paper over.

She took it and tucked it into the book on the table, watching as Jake made his way back through the curtains and into the bed-and-breakfast. She had just over two hours until Elijah's gallery opening tonight, and she needed to relax, but the name on the paper seared her memory.

It was part of her past that she'd stepped away from when she left New York. The part that held sad memories and bitter tears. She didn't want that to infiltrate her life, not even fifteen years later.

No, in this case, the past was best left right where it was. In the past.

16

"You look stunning!" Elijah said as she entered the cool air of the upscale gallery. The soft strains of classical music drifted through the air and the paintings fairly glowed in their specialized lighting.

"Thank you. And you look so handsome, Elijah. Are you ready for tonight?" There was still thirty minutes before the official opening and everything seemed to be in order, but he looked nervous.

"I—I think so?" He blushed and looked around the room. "I mean, I've done tons of exhibits before but nothing quite like this."

"Both of your styles meeting, you mean?"

"Yes. For some reason it makes me a little...uneasy."

"Why?" She stepped forward, camera in her hand.

"I think it's the fact that fans of both types of my work will be here. Before, they were separated, and it was easier. They seem to be very vocal about which is best."

He chuckled. "But now they'll be in the same space. It's overwhelming."

"And yet..." She held up a finger. "Think of it this way. They can see the progression—just like the way you set it up. If anyone has questions as to why you choose to paint one style or another, they can see that it's been evolving just as all art should. You change. Your art changes. No one can remain static."

He smiled, taking a deep breath and letting it out. "You know what? That's the best way anyone has ever described the transformation of art to me."

"I think it works for most transformations," she said, though she could feel her smile slipping as she thought about her own transformation and what she'd left behind. Everything felt fresh in her mind after seeing the name behind the emails.

"I'm sure you're right. Shall we get started?"

She nodded and they got to work. He explained the shots he was interested in seeing and she took them, encouraging him to stand in the middle of the gallery with both modern and impressionist on either side of him.

"That's it. Perfect!" she said as she slipped the camera into her bag. "Now to wait for the guests."

"Will we do?"

They turned to see Willard, Kay, Pete, Geraldine, and Vicky standing at the back entrance, all smiles and clearly excited for Elijah.

"Thank you, guys, for coming," he said, hugging them all.

"Couldn't let you start the night alone. This way you look as though you've got an entourage." Geraldine raised a hand with flair, and everyone laughed.

The gallery owner came in and pulled Elijah away for a few last-minute details, and Eva quickly filled the group in on what had happened with Paul.

"What a shame," Kay said.

"Good thing he's caught. You're not only saving birds, you might be saving more lives."

Eva shrugged. "It's sad, honestly. He did it all for money—or so I assume—but at least Beth's killer was captured, and we can truly celebrate tonight with no regrets."

They cheered and Elijah came back just as the screens went up at the front. The gallery officially opened, welcoming in his fans and curious newcomers who were about to discover their next favorite artist.

LATER THAT NIGHT, Eva felt a tap on her arm. She turned to see Jerome.

"You're here?" She couldn't help the quick glance over his sleek button up shirt, slacks, and open sport jacket. He looked different from when she saw him in a suit on the job, and she had to admit she liked the tilt his hair had at the front.

"I'm here. And you look…" He blinked, taking in her slim fitting black dress. "Beautiful."

It wasn't the word she'd expected. Perhaps nice or

lovely, but *beautiful?* It slipped past her defenses and rested against her heart, warming her cheeks at the attention.

"I, well, thank you. You look quite handsome yourself," she said, forcing a laugh after, but the way he looked at her was no laughing matter.

But then, as if realizing this himself, he looked around and reached for a glass of champagne from a waiter's tray. "This is a nice place."

"Are you much of an art fan, Detective Makos?"

"I am, Ms. Stewart."

They shared a smile.

"But I'll share a secret—when it comes to art, I know *when* I like something, but not necessarily *why*. I care more about the feeling I get from a piece than I do the artists or even the price tag."

"Interesting," she said, walking with him as he trailed to the impressionist side of Elijah's show.

"You may also find it interesting to note that Paul Hart made a full confession."

"He did?" she said, though too loudly, considering the sharp stares of a few couples near them.

"He did," Jerome said, the corner of his lips tilting upward. "It was like you said, he was bought off by smugglers and got used to the lifestyle. Or his *wife* got used to it. Our forensic accountant is looking into his background now, but it's been going on a while. He caught Beth snapping pictures of Lilly and Tim, and according to him, he snapped."

"That's what he said?"

"Yes. He seems genuinely repentant, but that doesn't discount what he did. He told us where to find her camera, and just from a quick glance at her shots, we have enough to stop the smuggling."

"That is good news," she said, feeling a peace rest over her. It didn't discount Beth's death, but somehow knowing that her work would help end the smuggling felt right.

Eva sighed and stopped in front of her favorite painting. The one she'd already purchased at the start of the exhibit. There was a discrete dot on the card that indicated it had been sold, but she'd allow it to stay for the duration of the installation so more people could enjoy it.

"Now this, this I like." He pointed to the painting.

"You do?"

"Yeah. I mean, I'd buy it...but not on a cop's budget." He chuckled.

"It's been taken," a short man with glasses said, butting into their conversation. He pointed at the name card. "That's what the dot means."

"Well, thanks." Jerome made a point of turning his back on the man, and Eva almost laughed.

"Anyway..." He glanced around to make sure the nosy man was gone. "I just wanted to say you did a good job. I...should have caught the issue with the breeding months not being right. Honestly, I think the other cases I'm working are wearing me thin."

"I'm just glad justice was served," she said, and she meant it.

"And, about your deal..." He paused and waited for her

to meet his vibrant green eyes. "You've earned yourself a consulting position—but on one condition."

Her heart pounded in her chest. It wasn't so much that she was desperate to consult, but she'd grown fond of solving cases with Jerome, and the thought of it never happening again put a damper on her mood.

"What is that?"

He waited, taking a sip of his champagne, clearly drawing it out for his own amusement.

"You are terrible," she said, wrinkling her nose at him. He laughed and then set his empty glass on a passing tray.

"On the condition you apply for a private investigator's license here in Florida."

It was the last thing she would have expected him to say. She'd envisioned him asking her to remain at home while he did the 'real' work or perhaps asking her not to involve the MMBC, but this was...perhaps worse.

Memories from her past rose up, reminding her of happy times as much as the sad. And then she remembered what she'd shared with him. Was he making this a condition in order to help her accomplish something that had been a long-past dream?

"I—I don't know."

His eyes narrowed, and he tilted his head to the side. "Think about it. It was once something you wanted, wasn't it? And if you want to discuss it further, we can. But for now, let's enjoy the art."

They moved on to the next set of paintings, and she listened as he talked about the ones he liked. His observations were humorous at some points but always right in line with her own thoughts. And slowly, she felt herself relax around him again.

Eventually, her thoughts trailed back to the emails and their sender, but she forced them away and refocused on memories of Uncle Sal again. The times she'd spent with him really had been some of the best of her young life. In Jerome's own way, he was offering her an opportunity to recapture some of what she'd lost after her uncle had died.

And maybe—just maybe—she'd take him up on that.

———

Check out the next mystery for the Murder Mystery Book Club, **The Hunt for Hemingway.**

Thanks for reading *On the Wings of Murder*. We hope you enjoyed this adventure with Eva Stewart, her book club, and, of course, Poirot the parrot. There are many more adventures coming your way. If you could take a minute and leave a review for me on Amazon and/or Goodreads, that would be really nice :)

The next story in the Florida Keys Bed & Breakfast Cozy Mystery series is called **The Hunt for Hemingway** and you can order it on Amazon.

If you would like to know about future cozy mysteries by me and the other authors at Fairfield Publishing, make sure to sign up for our Cozy Mystery Newsletter. We will send you our FREE Cozy Mystery Starter Library just for signing up. All the details are on the next page.

FAIRFIELD COZY MYSTERY NEWSLETTER

Make sure you sign up for the Fairfield Cozy Mystery Newsletter so you can keep up with our latest releases. When you sign up, **we will send you our FREE Cozy Mystery Starter Library!**

FairfieldPublishing.com/cozy-newsletter/

Made in the USA
Las Vegas, NV
27 June 2024